WILD TARGET

TYSON WILD BOOK THIRTY SIX

TRIPP ELLIS

D1212049

TRIPP ELLIS

1

The acrid smell of smoke filled the night air. Burned rubber, paint, interior fabric, and plastic swirled amid the soot and ash. Mixed with it was the disturbing, putrid stench that could only come from one source—burning flesh.

The fire department doused the flames, but there wasn't much left of the convertible Porsche—just blackened body panels and rims. The tires had melted into the asphalt. The charred body behind the wheel looked like a lump of coal in the vague shape of a human being—shriveled, cracked, and peeling, with wisps of smoke still seeping out.

The smoldering vehicle still crackled and hissed. The ground was coated with a slushy mix of water and ash. Red and blue lights flickered, and emergency personnel swarmed the area.

Dietrich, the forensic photographer, snapped photos. Brenda hovered over the remains. Arson investigators perused the burned-out shell of a vehicle. There wasn't much for the EMTs to do at this point.

Paris Delaney and her news crew arrived, and the camera lens started soaking up the gruesome scene. Our eyes connected for an instant. If there was death and destruction, Paris was never far behind.

It was just after 9 PM. The parking lot of the professional building was mostly empty. Just a few cars in random spaces. The stars flickered overhead, and a few clouds drifted with the breeze. It was a clear January night, and a bit of a cold front had rolled in—65° was a harsh winter for Coconut Key.

"Do we know who owns the car?" I asked.

Sheriff Daniels replied, "Michael Williams. *Dr. Michael Williams*. You know... the guy with the billboards."

I cupped my hands in front of my chest in the shape of sizable endowments.

"That's the one," Daniels remarked.

The two-story professional building was home to dentists, primary care physicians, pediatricians, a few acupuncturists, a medical massage therapy clinic, and the practice of Dr. Williams.

The island was plastered with billboards of stunning women with alluring enhancements, advertising the renowned plastic surgery clinic. Dr. Williams had earned the reputation as a skillful surgeon that could implant soft, supple assets virtually indistinguishable from the real thing. If you wanted the best boob job in town with minimal scarring, a natural feel, and the right amount of jiggle, Dr.

Williams was your man.

Of course, his handsome face and perfect smile appeared on every billboard alongside his alluring work. He looked like he belonged on a soap opera with his piercing blue eyes, square jaw, blindingly white teeth, and short brownish-blond wavy hair. In his mid-30s now, he looked like he could have been in a boy band in his teens.

Now he belonged in a horror movie.

Dr. Williams could sculpt perfect noses, do Brazilian butt lifts, and could enhance just about any part of your body that you felt was deficient. A tummy tuck, a chin implant, calf implants. You name it. You could also go in the opposite direction if you needed a reduction.

Lip fillers and Botox injections were a staple of his practice.

"Are we sure this is Dr. Williams?" I asked.

"The victim is male," Brenda said. "About the right size and build."

"Anybody see anything?"

The sheriff shook his head. "No security cameras either."

"I'm guessing he didn't set himself on fire," JD said.

"Who knows?" the sheriff groaned. "Maybe he got tired of his dull and boring life." His voice was thick with sarcasm.

"He didn't set himself on fire," Brenda said, hovering over the remains, wearing pink nitrile gloves. "I've got entry and exit wounds. Probably a small caliber pistol."

We drew closer, and she pointed out the small wounds in the head and neck. Left side entry, and a larger exit wound on the opposite side. "Looks like he was sitting in the seat when he was shot."

"Any shell casings found?" I asked.

"Not so far," a forensic investigator replied.

"An accelerant was used to facilitate the blaze," an arson investigator chimed in.

"So, somebody shot him, doused the car in gasoline, and set it on fire to cover their tracks," I said.

"I think that pretty much sums it up," Daniels muttered.

"Why?"

"That's your job to find out."

"Maybe somebody didn't like their new boobs," JD suggested.

Daniels gave him a look, and Jack just shrugged.

He probably wasn't far off.

Jack wasn't wearing his usual Hawaiian shirt. Today he was wearing an *I'm With Stupid* T-shirt, which wasn't my favorite in his beach bum couture collection.

"Do we know when this happened?" I asked.

"Hard to say. The body temperature is a little elevated," Brenda said dryly.

"Call came in about an hour ago," Daniels said. "A woman drove by and saw the fire."

"Was there anybody else in the building?"

"Doesn't appear that way."

"Anything stolen?" I asked.

"Victim doesn't have a watch," Brenda said. "I'll look for a wallet or money clip, but I'm not sure how much survived the fire."

"Has the next of kin been notified?"

"Again, your job," Daniels said.

It was my least favorite aspect of the job. "What was he doing here after hours?"

"Another good question," the sheriff said. "I suggest you two start looking for answers."

"You got it, boss."

The sheriff's eyes narrowed at me. As volunteers, the term *boss* annoyed him.

I walked to the main entrance and pulled the handle to the glass door. It was locked. There was no access without a key after hours. I dialed the number on the door for the property manager, but there was no answer. I left a voicemail, then rejoined Daniels and the others.

I surveyed the wretched scene for a moment, trying to visualize how it could have all played out. There was an empty parking space next to the incinerated Porsche. I noticed several cigarette butts on the asphalt by the yellow stripe. I directed a forensic investigator to bag them. "I'm thinking our killer parked next to the good doctor and sat in his car, smoking cigarettes, waiting for his target to come out. Then he shot Dr. Williams through an open window. That's why there are no shell casings. The ejections stayed in the vehicle. Let's run DNA on these cigarette butts and see if we can get a match from the database."

"We have no idea if those cigarettes belong to the killer," Daniels said.

"Worth a shot. It's all we've got."

"Something tells me this wasn't a random act," JD said. "This was a deliberate hit."

"Now, all we have to do is find out who wanted him dead."

Spouses are always suspects.

People often get the funny idea that murder is cheaper and more expedient than divorce. Sometimes it is, but murder always comes at a price. Even if you don't get caught, the burden always lingers—unless you're a true psychopath. Your victims haunt your dreams, show up in your nightmares, or stare back at you in the mirror.

You can't run from yourself.

You're stuck with the person you become. That's the divorce you can't get.

It was no surprise that Dr. Michael Williams lived in the posh neighborhood of *Stingray Bay*. Home of manicured lawns, cookie-cutter McMansions, and flashy cars. Everyone tried to keep up with everyone else. The *Joneses* did well in this neighborhood.

We pulled to the curb at 1134 Willow Bend Lane and strolled the walkway to the front door. The putrid stench of the crime scene still lingered in my nostrils—the image burned into my retina like a camera flash.

I rang the video doorbell.

A moment later, a woman's concerned voice answered. "Who is it?"

I flashed my badge to the camera lens and made introductions. "We'd like to talk to you about your husband."

"Is everything okay?"

"I think it's best if we talk face-to-face."

The light on the video doorbell went out. A few moments later, Megan Williams pulled open the door. She was an attractive blonde in her late 20s, wearing designer black pants and jacket, sparkling earrings, a diamond necklace, and big rocks on her perfectly manicured fingers. She had brown eyes, tan skin, and a trim figure. I expected the wife of a prominent plastic surgeon to be nothing less than a stunner, and she lived up to expectations.

"When was the last time you spoke with your husband?"

"This afternoon. Why? Is he okay?" she asked again, knowing something was wrong.

Deputies don't show up in the middle of the night asking about your husband if everything is okay.

"We found your husband's vehicle in the parking lot of his office building. It had been set on fire."

Her eyes rounded. "What about Austin?"

My brow knitted for an instant. "Your husband is Dr. Michael Williams, correct?"

She nodded, her eyes already beginning to mist. "Austin is his middle name. He always felt Michael was too common."

"We believe the person in the vehicle was your husband. But we don't have confirmation yet."

Megan clutched her fingers to her lips. She tried to screech, but no sound came out. Her eyes filled. "Are you saying he's dead?"

In as delicate a tone as possible, I said, "The medical examiner is trying to make a positive ID. Hopefully she can match dental records. Can you give me the name of your family dentist?"

She nodded, dazed. "Are you sure?"

I gave a grim nod. "Austin drives a red Porsche convertible, correct?"

She nodded, the tears rolling down her cheek now. The color drained from her face, and her knees wobbled. She clutched the door for support.

"Maybe you should sit down," I suggested.

She nodded, and I helped her through the foyer to the living room.

We'd been in several of the mansions in the neighborhood before, and while they all had unique touches, they shared common design elements—a large foyer with a staircase to the second floor. An office to the side of the foyer, opposite the parlor. A large living room with vaulted ceilings and plenty of windows. The patio pool glowed with light, and window lights from homes across the canal reflected on the water.

This home had marble tile in the foyer and bleached gray hardwoods in the living room. The walls were white, and colorful large canvases hung on the wall with teal and orange abstractions. It was an open floor plan that extended to the kitchen and bar.

I helped Megan to the white leather sofa, then sat next to her.

"What happened?"

I gave her the facts and a little bit of my theory. I think she heard about half of it, still in a daze.

"Do you need me to ID the remains?"

"I'm not sure if that's possible at this stage."

She gasped again, and her eyes widened.

"I know this is difficult, but time is of the essence. Can you think of anyone who may have wanted to harm your husband?"

She shook her head. In between sobs, she said, "No. Everybody loved Austin. He was just one of those guys. He could talk to anybody. Young, old, rich, poor. It didn't matter. You felt like he was on your level. That's why his patients loved him."

"Any disgruntled patients?"

"Not that I know of. I mean, you can't run a business without upsetting somebody. But he never mentioned anything to me. I really didn't get involved in the clinic. Work was work, and he always left the office at the office."

"Do you know why he was there late this evening?"

3

Megan's cell phone rang. She looked at the screen, then took the call. Her shattered voice uttered, "Hey Brandon."

Brandon's voice crackled through the speaker in her phone. It was loud enough for me to hear. "I just saw the news report. There was a car on fire, and it looked like—"

"I know," Megan said, breaking into sobs again.

"Is Austin okay?"

"They think he's dead." She could barely get the words out.

Brandon paused for a moment, speechless. "I'm so sorry. We'll be right over."

"Okay. Thank you." Megan ended the call and set the phone back on the glass coffee table near a fashion magazine.

She wiped her eyes as mascara stained her cheeks. I handed her a box of tissues from the coffee table. She grabbed a couple and blotted her eyes.

"That was Austin's best friend," she said after she regained her composure. She took a deep breath. "Is there any way this could be some kind of mistake?"

"We'll know more when the medical examiner makes a positive identification."

Megan snatched the phone from the coffee table again and dialed her husband. After a few rings, it went to voicemail. "Hey, it's me. I'm worried about you. I hope what they're saying isn't true. Call me right now. I don't care where you are or what you're doing."

She ended the call and sobbed again. Her head fell into her hands, and more tears streamed down her cheek. She was in the denial phase.

"You were about to tell me why Austin was at the office so late," I said.

She sniffled and wiped her eyes again. "He would often do after-hours work for friends or associates. Nothing major. Botox injections and fillers mostly. A lot of his guy friends were too vain to come in during the daytime, but they wanted something done about those wrinkles in their foreheads. It really does take years off your appearance."

"Do you know who he was working on?"

She shook her head. "He just said he'd be late at the office today. I didn't ask."

I paused for a moment, then asked in a delicate tone, "How was your relationship?"

"Great. Why?"

"Standard question."

"We were happy." She could barely hold it in as her eyes filled. Sobs and tears were about to burst out of her.

"How long have you been married?"

"Five years now. I can't believe it's gone by this fast."

"No problems?"

"I mean, we have our disagreements, like every couple. But no real problems. We communicate well. And our relationship has always been based on trust and honesty."

"You must be very trusting given the nature of his work."

Her face crinkled. "What do you mean?"

"I mean, I'm sure he encountered a lot of beautiful women in the course of his daily operations."

"You've seen one pair of tits—you've seen them all." She puffed up. "I have a good set. And they're real. I was never worried about the girls he met at the office."

She had a nice set indeed.

"I gave my husband no reason to stray if that's what you're getting at."

You'd have to be a fool to step out on Megan Williams. She lived up to the definition of a trophy wife.

"I'm sorry if these questions seem insensitive, but I'm sure you understand," I said. "We see a lot of crazy things."

"I'm sure you do. But I really can't think of anyone who might have wanted to kill my husband. You think this could have been a robbery gone wrong?"

"Does your husband wear a watch?"

She nodded. "A Rolex. Was it missing?"

"Yes."

"So, he *was* robbed?"

I shrugged. "Seems like a lot of trouble to go through to steal a watch."

"A $15,000 watch," she said. "And some people are desperate."

I'd seen people kill over $50 bucks. Nothing would surprise me anymore. "We'll keep an eye on the pawnshops. See if it turns up."

We talked more, and it wasn't long before the doorbell rang.

"Excuse me," Megan said as she lifted from the couch and scurried to the door. She let in Brandon and his wife, Kayla.

There were tearful hugs and condolences in the foyer. After they chatted briefly, she ushered them into the living room and made introductions.

Kayla sat on the couch with Megan, a consoling arm around her. The two friends sobbed.

Brandon Taylor had a slew of questions. *What happened? How? When? Why?*

All good questions and things I liked to hear. I grew suspicious when people didn't ask about the details. I went over everything with him.

Brandon was an average-looking guy in his mid 30s with a round face and a small spare tire around the midsection. His hair was thinning on top, and he had a short beard that accentuated his jawline on his otherwise round face. He had narrow brown eyes, and his skin was a little red around the cheeks and nose. He looked like the kind of guy that burned easily in the sun.

His wife, Kayla, was out of his league. WAY out of his league. I figured Brandon had money. He lived a few houses down, and these addresses weren't cheap.

Kayla was late 20s with midnight hair, sapphire eyes, and sculpted cheekbones. Her full lips just begged for attention, and it wasn't hard to imagine the naughty nothings that could slip from them, given the right circumstances. Her tight yoga pants and a sports bra highlighted her breathtaking figure.

Thank God for yoga pants.

I asked Brandon if he could think of anybody that had any animosity toward Austin. He gave me the same story as Megan, describing Austin as a likable guy that everyone admired. And maybe that was part of the problem. Austin had everything. Sometimes envy breeds contempt. Maybe he had too much, and somebody just wanted to level the playing field.

"Where were you this evening?" I asked, trying to sound casual.

4

"I was at home, watching TV with the kids," Brandon said. "Kayla was at yoga."

"How many children do you have?" I asked.

"Two, from a previous marriage."

"Where are they now?"

"At home, in bed. I should probably get back."

"How old are they?"

"Seven and nine. Little hell raisers. I'll be lucky if the house is still standing."

"I understand. Just a few more questions before you go. Can you think of anyone who had a vendetta against Dr. Williams?"

Brandon sucked his teeth and shook his head. "I really can't. This is just a total shock to me."

I dug into my pocket and gave him my card. "Get in touch if you can think of anything that might be helpful."

Brandon nodded. He offered his condolences once again to Megan and exchanged a glance with his wife.

"I'll probably spend the night here with Megan," Kayla said, then looked at Megan for confirmation. "If you don't want to be alone."

Megan nodded. "Would you?"

"You know we're both here for you," Kayla said. "Whatever you need."

The girls cried and hugged each other again.

Brandon excused himself.

We asked a few more questions. Before we left, I told Megan I'd be in touch and would update her as soon as Brenda matched the dental records.

We strolled the walkway and hopped into JD's lava orange Porsche convertible. He cranked up the engine, and it growled with possibilities. "Something's funny about this."

I agreed. "I'll have Denise dig into Austin's social media profiles and check the online reviews."

"Like I said, maybe somebody with a botched boob job took revenge."

He pulled away from the curb, and we headed back to the station to fill out after-action reports. I texted Brenda the contact information for Austin's dentist. She could call in the morning and pull records. Then I called Isabella, my handler at Cobra Company. "I need another favor."

Cobra Company was a private clandestine agency with unparalleled intelligence resources. Isabella had a treasure trove of data at her fingertips. How she acquired the data wasn't always legal and couldn't be used in a court of law. But it could tell us where to focus our attention.

"You only call me when you want something."

"That's not true," I protested half-heartedly.

She was silent for a moment. It was true. A resigned sigh escaped her lips. "Who do you want me to track?"

I gave her the address of the professional building and asked her to work her magic and see if any cell phones were pinging the nearby tower at the time of Dr. Williams's murder.

"I'll give it a look and get back to you," she said. "It's a little hectic right now."

"Everything okay?"

"Nothing I can't handle. Ciao for now."

She ended the call.

It was almost midnight when we stopped in *Diver Down* and had a drink at the bar. Teagan greeted us with a bubbly smile behind the counter. The teal-eyed beauty was always a refreshing sight in her bikini top and jean shorts. She'd seen Paris Delaney's story on the news, and we fielded a few questions while she served us two glasses of fine whiskey.

"I see that guy's commercials all the time," Teagan said. "They ran one right after Paris Delaney's report. Kind of ironic, huh?"

"I know who did it," Harlan shouted from his perch at the end of the bar.

I gave the old Marine a skeptical glance. "Oh yeah? Who?"

"You know, it just slipped my mind. The old brain ain't what it used to be," he said, tapping his noggin. "But another drink might jog my memory," he said, wiggling his empty longneck.

I rolled my eyes. He was just angling for a free beer. "Were you a witness? Did you see it happen?"

"He's been sitting here all evening," Teagan said.

Harlan scowled at her playfully. "Don't blow my cover."

Teagan gave him a sassy look.

"What's your theory, Devil Dog?" I asked.

"I bet I could solve this thing faster than you numbskulls."

"Talk to Sheriff Daniels. He might deputize you," I joked.

"Hell, this place could use a real deputy."

I rolled my eyes, then nodded to Teagan. She pulled a long neck out of the well, snatched the bottle opener from her back pocket, twirled it around, and popped the top in a fluid motion. The bottle hissed, and the cap fell away. She slid the beer down the counter to Harlan.

He grinned and gave a nod of appreciation as he tipped the bottle in our direction. "Much obliged." He took a refreshing swig. "There's another serial killer on the island, picking off rich assholes. That's my take."

"By all accounts, Dr. Williams was a nice guy," I said.

"Looks can be deceiving. Not everything is as it seems. Especially around here."

"I hope there's not another serial killer running around," Teagan muttered.

"I don't think you have anything to worry about," I assured. "This was a targeted attack. There wasn't anything random about it."

We hung out for a few drinks and shot the shit, theorizing about the case. Harlan shared his opinion, whether anyone wanted to hear it or not. He had all kinds of outlandish conspiracies concocted in his mind. But in this town, outlandish conspiracies weren't much of a stretch. Something about the sunshine, the clean air, the teal water, the pristine beaches, and the beautiful women drew people from all over, looking to start fresh and make something of themselves. It drew ambitious entrepreneurs and shady grifters alike. The island was paradise. The land of opportunity. All it took was a dream and ambition. Some people just happened to have dreams of drugs and murder.

It was almost 2 AM by the time we had solved all the world's problems. But we were just a couple of guys in a bar, and I was pretty sure our solutions would fall on deaf ears.

JD went home, and I ambled down the dock to the *Avventura*. I crossed the passerelle to the superyacht and was greeted by an excited Jack Russell. I grabbed Buddy's leash, took him for a walk, then settled in for the evening.

Brenda called in the morning. The phone buzzed the nightstand next to the bed. I reached a sleepy hand to grab it, swiped the screen, and held the phone to my ear. I croaked, "Tell me something good."

"I was able to pull a 9mm slug from the remains. It was lodged in the collarbone. The other bullet must have made a clean exit through the other side of his skull. The forensics guys never did find it. I'll run ballistics and see if I can find a match in the system." She paused. "Oh, and there's more bad news."

5

———

"**H**ave you talked to Daniels this morning?" Brenda asked.

"Not yet," I said.

"He'll be calling any minute."

My phone buzzed with another call. "That's him now. We'll talk soon."

I clicked over and took the call. "I was just talking to Brenda. What's up?"

"Missing girl. 17. Name is Zoe Brooks. I need you and numbnuts to talk to her mother. Figure out if Zoe just ran off or if we're going to find her floating in a canal."

I groaned. "Hell of a way to start off the new year."

"You're telling me."

Daniels texted me the address for Grace Brooks and sent a picture of Zoe. She was a beautiful young girl with blue eyes and long sandy brown hair with just a slight wave. She was a fresh-faced kid that could have done ads for skin cleansers. Pouty lips and eyes that held mystery and promise.

I called JD and caught him up to speed, then pulled myself out of bed, showered, and grabbed breakfast. He swung by the marina in the Porsche and picked me up 15 minutes later. We zipped across the island to 2322 Sailfish Court.

Grace lived in a narrow white house with sky blue shutters. A white picket fence surrounded a 3x10 area that was the yard. Palm trees and ferns sprouted skyward. A brick driveway ran along the side of the house, gated by a white fence.

We parked at the curb, crossed the sidewalk, and climbed the steps to the porch. A frazzled Grace Brooks answered after I knocked. She was mid 30s with long platinum blonde hair, aided by the help of a salon. Grace had the same blue eyes as Zoe. She was an attractive woman—5'3" with creamy skin and a few more curves than she would have liked. Hopelessness filled her face.

I flashed the badge and made introductions.

"Please, come in."

It was a two-bedroom, two-bath house with 920 square feet. Grey hardwoods, white walls, and tasteful modern furniture. The kitchen was tiny with natural wood siding, mint green countertops, and older appliances.

Grace offered us a seat on the gray-cloth sofa. A steamer trunk on top of a throw rug served as a coffee table. A 42-inch flatscreen was perched atop an entertainment center along the wall.

"When was the last time you saw your daughter?" I asked.

"It's been over a month now."

I lifted an incredulous brow. "And you're just now reporting her missing?"

"It's complicated." Grace sighed. "I've been having a lot of trouble with Zoe lately. I'm doing the best I can, but this single-parent thing isn't easy." Her eyes brimmed.

"And she got into a phase where she just wouldn't listen to me."

"They do that," JD said.

"I knew she was dabbling with drugs here and there. Then I caught her with some in the house, and that was the last straw. I said she was not going to do that under my roof, and as long as she was living here, she would have to abide by my rules. Well, she threw that back in my face and said she was leaving. She took her things and moved in with that loser boyfriend of hers."

"What's his name?" I asked.

"Axel Everhart," she said.

"Do you have address and contact information for him?"

"I had his phone number, but it no longer works. I thought about cutting off Zoe's phone when she left, but then I wouldn't have a way to get in touch with her, so I kept paying the bill. And at least I could look at the statement and see that she was making and receiving calls." Grace took a breath. "I would send her texts, and occasionally she would reply that she was okay. But that all stopped last week. I haven't heard anything from her. She won't return my messages. And there's been no activity on the phone."

"She could be using another device," I said. "It's possible that her boyfriend has convinced her to drop contact with you. It's not uncommon. We'll track him down and see if we can locate her. You have a recent picture of Zoe?"

She nodded and scrolled through her phone. I gave her my contact info, and she texted a few pictures. One was a school picture where Zoe looked fresh-faced. The other was more recent. She had a pink stripe in her hair and heavy eyeliner. She looked annoyed and hollow. It was almost like looking at two different girls.

"Please tell me she's okay," Grace pleaded in a shaky voice.

"I'm sure she's fine. Most of the time, people turn up within a few days."

"I'm just so worried about her. I can't sleep. I keep dreaming she's going to turn up dead with a needle in her arm."

"Was she doing the hard stuff?"

"I know she was smoking weed and doing molly. I told her you don't know where this stuff is coming from or what's in it. I was watching a show that said half the molly on the street is just speed, or worse."

Molly was slang for MDMA, otherwise known as Ecstasy. But pure, high-quality MDMA was hard to come by these days. Most of it was some type of amphetamine, often cut with fentanyl. That was a recipe for disaster.

"What can you tell me about Axel?" I asked.

"He's older. I think early 20s... 22, 23 maybe."

"And you were okay with that?"

"What choice did I have? If I told her not to do something, she'd double down on it."

"Do you know where Axel works?"

"I think Zoe said he was a bartender, but I don't know where."

"We'll figure it out," I said. "What about friends?"

"Well, she was best friends with Natalie Novak. Really sweet girl. Beautiful. Smart. Funny. But ever since she started seeing Axel, it seems like he's isolated her."

"That's a common pattern among abusers. Narcissistic personality types. They can control their victims better once they isolate them."

Grace frowned.

"You know if she was still going to school?"

"I don't think so. I got several calls about her attendance. I said she was no longer living in the house, and I had no control over her behavior." A desperate sigh escaped her lips. "Please find my baby."

I assured Grace we'd do everything possible.

We finished up, and Grace escorted us to the door. We said our goodbyes, and she watched from the doorway as we walked to the Porsche. My first call was to Denise as I climbed inside the vehicle. JD cranked up the engine and pulled away from the curb.

"Hey, doll. I need you to do me a favor."

"Whatever you need."

"Careful, I might take that the wrong way."

"Maybe I meant it the wrong way," she sassed.

"Tease."

She scoffed.

"What can you tell me about Axel Everhart?"

6

"DUI, possession of marijuana," Denise said. "That's it. According to DMV records, he's got a brand new Corvette registered in his name. The guy must do pretty well for himself. I'll text you his current address."

"Thank you," I said.

"Anything else?"

"Pull cell records for Michael Austin Williams. See if anything unusual stands out."

"You got it."

I ended the call and told JD to drive to the high school. I figured we could pull Natalie Novak from class and have a word with her before tracking down Axel.

We turned into the faculty parking lot, and Jack found an isolated space, trying to keep his new Porsche free of door dings. I'm not sure how successful the strategy was. No matter how far away you parked, somebody would always park next to you. We hopped out of the car and ambled toward the main building. The lights flashed as JD clicked the alarm.

We pushed through the double doors and strolled the empty hallways to the main office. Class was in session, so we avoided student traffic.

I flashed my badge to Mrs. Garrett in the principal's office and asked to speak with Natalie Novak. Mrs. Garrett was early 60s with grayish-brown curly hair and a frumpy figure.

"Is she in some kind of trouble?" she asked from behind the counter.

"No, ma'am. We just need to question her in the disappearance of Zoe Brooks."

Her eyes rounded, and she gasped. "Oh no! I hope Zoe's okay."

"When was the last time Zoe attended class?"

Mrs. Garrett's fingers clacked the keyboard. She looked down her nose through her bifocals. Her brown eyes surveyed the screen. "Looks like she hasn't been to class in over a month." Her fingers danced across the keys again. "Natalie is currently in government class. I can send an office assistant to fetch her."

"That would be great."

She grabbed a form, filled it out, and handed it to a student assistant who dashed out of the office. The kid was happy to stretch his legs. He returned 10 minutes later with Natalie.

I flashed my badge and made introductions, then asked Mrs. Garrett if there was somewhere private we could talk. She directed us to a nearby conference room that was empty, and we stepped inside with Natalie and took a seat at the table.

"When was the last time you had any contact with Zoe?" I asked.

Golden ringlets of hair framed her adorable face. She had bright blue eyes and a pearly smile. Natalie was the kind of girl that everyone adored, and she never met a stranger. Bubbly and vivacious. She looked like a pageant queen. "Zoe hasn't been to class in a while."

"Her mother tells us you two used to be best friends."

Natalie nodded.

"But you haven't talked recently?"

"We drifted apart. She started hanging out with the wrong crowd."

"Axel?"

She nodded again. "I like to have fun as much as anybody else, but Zoe was having too much fun, if you know what I mean."

"Drugs?"

"And I'm not just talking a little weed."

"She was getting the drugs from Axel?"

"Yeah. I mean, she wasn't doing this stuff before she met him. That wasn't our thing. Don't get me wrong, we'd sneak beers here and there. A little vodka and cranberry. But this is high school. You're supposed to drink and have a good time."

"You're supposed to get an education and prepare for college."

She looked at me flatly. "Yeah, that too. But these are prime fun years before responsibility sets in. And you know what they say, all work and no play..."

"You know how she met Axel?"

"At the Helm Station. He's a bartender."

"And what were you girls doing at the Helm Station?"

She paused. "Did I say I ever went to the Helm Station?"

Natalie was a smart girl.

"You're not going to get in trouble," I assured.

"I can neither confirm nor deny that we *may* have used fake IDs."

"Where did you get the fake IDs?"

"I don't recall." She smiled, then leaned in and whispered, "Newsflash. You don't really need an ID to get into a lot of places. It's amazing what a little makeup and a pushup bra can do."

I dug into my pocket and slid a card across the table. "If you hear anything from Zoe, call me right away."

"You don't think something happened to her, do you?" she asked, concern suddenly filling her eyes.

I shrugged. "I don't know. Maybe she's just gone radio silent. Maybe she skipped town, went on some adventure. Did she ever mention to you any places she wanted to see?"

"Oh, yeah. For sure. When we were close, we always talked about going to Europe. We wanted to go to France, Spain, Portugal, and Italy. We used to plan all these crazy adventures that we were going to go on after high school." She frowned. "It makes me sad. Sucks when you lose a friend."

"Did you ever voice your opinion about Axel and her new lifestyle choices?"

"Yeah, I told her all the time I didn't think he was good for her. But all that did was push her away. And I didn't want to be around the guy. I'm not comfortable around people doing drugs. Like I said, drinking is one thing. Sticking needles in your vein is another."

"So she *was* doing the hard stuff?"

"Yeah." Natalie sighed. "It's really tragic." She paused. "You know, it's so crazy. I used to tell her if she kept doing what she was doing, that she'd probably OD in some seedy motel room and the cops would come around asking me questions about her whereabouts. Now here you are." Her eyes rounded. "You don't think she's dead, do you?"

"I sure hope not."

Natalie frowned.

"I guess we should let you get back to class."

"There's only ten minutes left. Can't you think of more questions? I don't want to go back."

7

We left the high school and headed across the island. Axel lived in the *Coconut Club* apartments. The units were two-story walk-ups with uncovered lot parking. They had gray siding and pitched roofs with tall palms dotting the property. The complex surrounded a sprawling pool with lounge chairs and a barbecue grill. Not a bad place for a 22-year-old kid. The rent wasn't cheap.

There was no security gate on the property. We pulled into the parking lot, hopped out, and strolled the concrete path that snaked between the units, looking for apartment C207. We climbed the switchback staircase, and I put a heavy fist into the door.

A moment later, a muffled voice shouted, "Who is it?"

"Coconut County. Open up!"

There was a moment's hesitation, then the deadbolt unlatched and the door creaked as Axel pulled it open. He looked quite a bit different from his DMV photo. His short brown hair was now platinum blond, almost white. He was a skinny guy with angular features, blue eyes, and high cheekbones. He had a little stubble in the shape of a goatee —it was the only place he could grow it. Tattoos crept up his neck from his collar. His arms were sleeved with mono-chrome ink. He looked like he belonged in an indie pop-punk band.

I flashed my badge. "We're looking for Zoe Brooks."

He shrugged and shook his head. "Haven't seen her."

"You haven't seen her today? Or you haven't seen her in a while?"

"A while."

"I was told she lived here."

"Not anymore."

"When did she move out?" I asked, suspicious.

"A little over a week ago."

"What happened? You two break up?"

His face crinkled. "What!? No. We weren't a thing. I just let her stay here. She was having trouble at home."

"You weren't dating?"

"No. We were just friends."

"That's not what her mother says."

He scoffed. "I don't care what her mother says."

"So you weren't engaged in a sexual relationship with Zoe Brooks."

His face crinkled again. "No. Dude, she's way too young for me."

He was clearly lying.

"Right," I said in a dry, incredulous tone, my eyes piercing into his. "So you just let her stay here out of the goodness of your heart."

He nodded. "Basically."

"Did she say where she was going when she moved out?"

"No."

"What prompted the move?"

"I told her she could stay here for a little while until she figured out a permanent solution. I guess she figured out a permanent solution."

"And you don't know what that solution is?"

He shook his head. "I didn't ask."

"You know how to get in touch with her?"

"She didn't leave a forwarding address," he snarked.

I wanted to smack the guy. "What about a phone number?"

"Sorry. Can't help you."

"What about the phone her mother paid for? She hasn't used it recently. Did she have another phone?"

"I don't know. I didn't pay much attention." He paused as we stared him down. "You know, she did mention wanting to go up north. She said something about trying to be a model in New York."

It was another line of bullshit.

Zoe was a pretty girl, but at 5'4" tall, she wasn't going to be a fashion model. That didn't keep plenty of shorter girls from trying. And there were other types of modeling. But fashion in NYC, not so much.

"So, she just up and left?" I asked.

"Yeah. She couldn't stay here forever."

"Mind if we come inside and take a look around?"

"You got a warrant?"

"I can get one."

"Then get one."

"You know, I get suspicious when people get defensive."

His face twisted again. "I'm not defensive. I get suspicious when cops don't want to respect my fourth amendment rights."

"It doesn't concern you that Zoe is missing?"

"Zoe is not missing. I'm sure she's out having fun with her friends somewhere, living a carefree, adventurous life."

"I hope so." We stared at each other for a moment. "What about drugs? Did you see her do any drugs while she lived here?"

"I just say *no* to drugs."

I looked at his arms but didn't see any telltale track marks. But users get pretty good about finding obscure locations to shoot up. I'd seen junkies shoot just about everywhere—

between their toes, their feet, legs, abdomen, neck. Use heroin long enough, and it will start to collapse the veins, and you'll have no choice but to get creative with where you inject your poison. Eventually, you'll get *shot out* with no usable veins—a dreaded place to be for any junky.

Axel was skinny, but I couldn't say for certain if he was *heroin skinny*. He didn't look doped up at the moment. His eyes were clear, and he was lucid. Maybe he was just an enabler.

I gave him a card, though I knew it was pointless. "If you hear from Zoe, contact me. Her mother is really worried about her."

He scoffed. "Her mother doesn't care about her."

"And you do?"

"I want the best for her. I gave her a place to stay, didn't I?"

"Maybe you gave her a little more than that," JD said.

Axel's eyes narrowed at him. "I think I'm done talking to you guys."

He closed and latched the door.

"He's definitely the kind of guy I'd want my daughter to date," JD quipped as we walked away. "How do you think he pays for the car and the apartment?"

8

"Maybe he makes good tips," I joked.

I didn't buy Axel's BS for a second. It was clear to me he had a little side hustle going on, probably involving drugs. I figured a stakeout might be in order to get a better picture of what he was into.

My mind swirled with possibilities. That sinking feeling twisted in my stomach. Axel knew exactly where Zoe Brooks was. Perhaps at the bottom of the ocean or in a shallow grave. Maybe he fed her drugs, and she OD'd. Who knows? I hoped I was wrong. But that little voice in my head told me I probably wasn't far from the truth.

We headed back to the professional building to talk to the office staff at the plastic surgery clinic. The building lobby had an atrium with Koi ponds and fountains. Skylights illuminated the area. Switchback staircases and a glass elevator led up to the second floor. Dr. Williams's clinic was located in suite #201 and took up a quarter of the floor. A large practice.

Susan Hammond was on the phone canceling appointments for the day when we stepped into the waiting room. She looked frazzled and overwhelmed.

Austin's physician's assistant, Aubrey Benson, called clients as well.

I flashed my badge at the counter.

Susan quickly ended her call and greeted us. She was a round woman with short auburn hair that dangled above her shoulders. She had pretty baby blue eyes with heavy liner.

"Busy day?" I asked.

"There are four months of appointments I need to cancel."

"Dr. Williams booked up pretty far in advance?"

She nodded. "It's just terrible. I can't believe it. Do you have any leads?"

"Not yet."

"If there's anything we can do to help," Susan said.

Aubrey nodded in agreement, listening in on our conversation as she spoke on the phone with a client. She was an attractive woman in her late 30s with golden hair that hung to her white lab coat. She had smoldering blue eyes, a perfect nose, plump lips, and eye-catching augmentations.

"I put a call into the property manager but haven't heard back," I said.

"The landlord sucks. Nothing gets fixed around here. I've been telling Dr. Williams he needed to move his practice out of this building, but the rent was cheap, and he liked the space. I mean, nothing's cheap on the island, but relatively speaking."

"Do you have any idea what Austin was doing here after hours last night?"

"I left around 5:30 PM. He said he was gonna stay and catch up on some things."

Aubrey ended her call and joined the conversation. "He told me he was going to stick around and have a Botox party with some of his friends."

"Was that pretty common?"

The two girls exchanged a glance.

"Maybe once or twice a month," Aubrey said. "Dr. Williams had a lot of friends."

"Guy friends? Girlfriends?"

The girls exchanged another glance.

"Dr. Williams was a wonderful family man," Susan said. "In all the years that I worked for him, never once did he make an inappropriate comment or even seem interested in other women."

His PA nodded. "If he *did* have female clients after hours, it was strictly business."

"Why not conduct business during normal hours?" I asked.

"Dr. Williams liked to barter," Aubrey said. "Botox injections for his wife's personal masseuse. Lip filler for the sales lady who sold him his new car. That kind of thing."

"Did he have any enemies? Disgruntled clients?"

Susan and the PA exchanged another glance.

Aubrey said with confidence, "I've never seen a client that didn't have an improved result."

Susan cleared her throat, and Aubrey gave her a curious glance.

"Lydia Keller," Susan muttered.

A wave of recognition washed over Audrey's face. "You're right." She cringed.

I said, "I take it that Lydia had a less than positive outcome with Dr. Williams?"

"I can't directly discuss individual patient outcomes, you understand," Aubrey replied. "But let's just say we did have one client last year that got an infection after a reduction. I don't think it was necessarily the fault of Dr. Williams. These things happen. And sometimes, patients don't handle wound care properly. The nipple turned necrotic, and there was nerve damage as well. I believe this particular individual lost sensation in the area as well as needing a complete reconstruction. If I'm not mistaken, she went elsewhere to have that done."

"Was there a malpractice suit?"

"There were plenty of angry phone calls, and I believe she showed up at the office on a few occasions to express her displeasure. Dr. Williams offered to do what he could to remedy the situation, but she refused any further treatment from this facility. It was just a terrible situation all the way around. She felt disfigured, and rightfully so. But infection is one of the risks, and patients sign off on these things before they undergo an elective procedure."

"So basically, the patient signs their life away and has no recourse," JD grumbled.

"The patient would have recourse if the doctor acted negligently, but he didn't. There are risks inherent with every procedure."

"You think this person was upset enough to take revenge?"

The girls exchanged another look.

"If this would have happened at the time, I would have said *yes*," Aubrey replied. "But that was a year ago. It seems a little delayed, don't you think? I mean, I almost forgot about it."

"I don't think Lydia's forgotten about it," I said.

"I think said person is worth looking into," Susan added.

I made note of the patient's name in my phone. "Can you think of anyone else?"

The girls shook their heads.

"What about drugs?"

"Are you asking if Dr. Williams used drugs?" Aubrey asked.

I nodded.

"No."

"I'll say it again. Dr. Williams was a family man," Susan said.

"What about gambling? Did he owe anybody any money?"

"I can't really speak to Dr. Williams's personal business," Aubrey said. "But I don't think he was hurting for cash. He charged a premium, and we were booked up months in advance. Plus he was a shrewd investor."

"I guess you both are out of a job now," I said.

The girls frowned.

"We'll wind things down here, then I'm not sure what the future holds," Aubrey said.

Sadness filled their eyes.

I thanked them for their time and gave the ladies my card before we left.

My phone buzzed with a text from Isabella as we reached JD's Porsche. *[No cell phones were in the area at the time of Dr. Williams's murder.]*

I thanked her for the info. Our killer was smart enough to turn off any devices he or she may have been carrying.

We climbed into the car, and Jack cranked up the engine. He headed toward Oyster Avenue to grab lunch. Afterward, I called Denise and asked her to dig up information on Lydia Keller. I figured she was worth talking to.

Denise's fingers danced across the keys as she pulled Lydia's records. "Hmm. Well, this is sad."

9

"Lydia Keller is deceased," Denise said.

I lifted a surprised brow.

"Official cause of death is listed a suicide."

I cringed. "When?"

"Three months ago."

"I guess we can cross her off the suspect list."

"Not so fast. She is survived by a son. Cody Keller. Lives in Sunset Park."

I theorized, "Lydia has a botched job, ends up disfigured, commits suicide over it, and her son takes revenge."

"Could be."

"Send me the address."

"You got it," she said before ending the call.

The text buzzed through a moment later. I showed the address to JD, and he made a face.

"Do we really have to go there?" he joked.

"We can take a cab over there if you prefer," I said.

Almost every time we went to *Sunset Park*, something bad happened to Jack's car. He was a little extra cautious with his new ride. Jack contemplated the suggestion for a moment but continued on to *Sunset Park,* anyway.

We pulled into the lot, and JD found an empty space with no surrounding cars. He gave a cautious glance around as we hopped out. There were no kids playing baseball, no suspicious characters loitering around, no imminent dangers to the car. He clicked the alarm, and the lights flashed.

We marched to a single-wide trailer, climbed the creaky wooden steps to the porch, and banged on the door.

The homes in *Sunset Park* ran the gamut. There were several nice, well-maintained trailers with pristine latticework around the base, colorful rose gardens, and well-manicured lawns. Others were rusted and dilapidated, sitting amid a jungle of weeds.

Cody's trailer fell somewhere in the middle.

"Who is it?" a voice shouted from within. Heavy footsteps rumbled toward the door.

"Coconut County," I barked. "We'd like to ask you a few questions."

"You got a warrant?"

"We're just here to talk. Why would we need a warrant?"

There was no response.

A moment later, Cody pulled open the door with a quizzical look on his face. His hazel eyes looked us up and down, and he seemed even more confused by our appearance.

Cody was early 20s, with short blonde spiky hair. He had narrow eyes, a square jaw, and smooth skin. He was fit and stood about 6 feet tall. He wore a T-shirt, jeans, and sneakers. He had a rebellious look in his eyes and looked like he did well with the ladies.

"You guys are cops?" he asked, skeptical.

I let him look at my badge.

"You don't look like cops." His eyes flicked between the two of us. He pointed at JD. "You. I recognize you."

"I get that a lot."

Cody's face crinkled. "Where do I know you from?"

JD shrugged modestly.

I tried to steer the conversation back on track. "We'd like to talk to you about your mother."

His face went long. "What's there to talk about?"

"I know this is a painful subject, but can you tell me what happened?"

His annoyed eyes glared at me. "She blew her fucking head off. That's what happened."

"I'm sorry," I said in a sincere tone.

"You want to see where she did it?" He pointed to the couch in the living room. "She sat down right there, put the barrel of the shotgun in her mouth, and used her foot to pull the trigger. There was blood and brains all over the wall." His face reddened, and his eyes misted. He seethed with anger. "You know what it's like to clean up something like that? Picking up pieces of your mom, prying bits of bone and flesh off the wall?"

There was nothing either of us could say.

"I had to get new carpet, a new couch, and repaint the walls. I can't stand it here, but I have nowhere else to go at the moment."

"Did she leave a note?" I asked.

"She didn't have to. It was pretty obvious. Why are you guys here, anyway? Coconut County already investigated this. Do I need a lawyer?"

"Did you do something that would require the services of a lawyer?"

His face twisted into a scowl. "No. But that didn't stop those jackasses from investigating me. At first, they tried to say I killed her. Said she couldn't have reached the trigger with the shotgun in her mouth. I had to point out to the dipshit deputies that she had taken her shoe off and pulled the trigger with her big toe."

"Did this have something to do with her medical issues?"

"You mean the fact that she was butchered by that asshole?"

I nodded.

"You're goddamn right. That bastard mutilated her. Her life was never the same. She saved up for so long to be able to afford his fee. They ought to take away that guy's license. She tried to get herself repaired, but that only made things worse. She was in constant pain. She lost all sensation. She went into a terrible depression. My stepdad left her. She felt like she was never going to find anybody to love her for who she was." His eyes filled. A tear rolled down his cheek. He didn't sob or cry, but his eyes flowed. "You know what the worst part is? I gotta see that bastard's face on billboards all over town."

"You know he's dead, right?"

Cody lifted his surprised brow. "No. I didn't know that."

"He was shot Wednesday night in the parking lot of his professional building, then torched."

A smirk curled Cody's lips. "Serves him right."

"You own a gun?"

"I got a few. Why?" he asked with suspicious eyes.

"9mm?"

"Yeah?"

"Mind if we take a look at it?"

"Go fuck yourself."

"Where were you Wednesday evening between 7 and 8 PM?"

Anger welled in his face. His eyes flicked between the two of us. "Eat shit. I'm not playing this game."

He slammed the door.

JD and I exchanged a glance. We descended the steps and headed back toward the Porsche.

"I'd say he's got some anger issues," Jack said.

"Understandably so."

JD clicked the alarm, and the lights flashed as we returned to the Porsche. It had survived the excursion to *Sunset Park*.

We hopped in, and he cranked up the engine, pulled out of the space, and drove across the lot to the exit.

A red Super Duty squealed around the corner, entering the park. The truck's bumper came millimeters from side-swiping the Porsche.

Jack honked the horn, shouted a few obscenities at the guy, and gave an unmistakable gesture with his middle finger.

With his window down, the burly truck driver heard every word.

The tires locked up, and the driver's door flung open. He put the vehicle in park, hopped out with an iron pipe in hand, and stormed toward the Porsche with an angry scowl on his face.

JD jumped out, and I followed, flashing my badge.

I recognized the guy right away, and he recognized us. We'd had a run-in with the burly guy before.

Cooter groaned. "You again."

"Watch where you're going," JD admonished.

Cooter stared us down for a moment, then backed off, tossed the pipe back into the cab, and raised his hands innocently. "My bad. I'll slow down."

After his last arrest, I don't think he wanted any more trouble.

He climbed back into the truck and found a place to park.

We continued on our way, and I sent Isabella a text asking her to get the location data for Cody Keller's cell phone the night of Austin's murder.

We decided to hit Dowling Street, looking for Zoe Brooks. It was the seedier part of town where you could find someone to fulfill your illicit desires. The street corners offered everything from drugs to prostitution and were full of runaways and people with nowhere else to turn.

If Zoe was still alive, addicted to heroin, and on her own, Dowling Street might be a good place to look.

10

W e cruised the boulevard with the top down, driving slowly. I surveyed the corners and the alleyways. All you had to do was slow down and pull to the curb. Someone would soon appear, hustling their goods. A lava orange Porsche prowling this part of town could only mean one thing—somebody looking for a good time.

JD pulled to the corner at the intersection of Carver and Dowling. Two young ladies in faux leather miniskirts and high heels strolled toward the vehicle, their tube tops bouncing, their fake nails sparkling. One was a brunette, the other was a bottle blonde, both in their mid 20s.

"Hey Sugar, I know exactly what you need," the blonde said.

I chuckled.

"And she ain't it," the brunette quipped. "What you want, only Raven can give you."

The blonde's face crinkled. "Bitch, I saw him first!"

"Ladies, there's no need to fight," I said with a smile.

"Oh, so you think you can handle us both?"

"Hello, do they not see me in the car?" JD muttered.

"Oh, I see you, Honey," the blonde said. "But if it's all the same, Champaign wants to show your friend a good time."

"Actually, I'm looking for someone in particular," I said.

Their faces crinkled.

I displayed a picture of Zoe on my phone.

The girls surveyed the screen. Their cheap perfume overpowered my nostrils as they leaned close.

Champaign said, "So you like them young?"

"She's missing. Her mother's worried about her. Have either of you seen her recently?"

"Sorry, Sugar," Champagne said. "I ain't seen her." She looked at Raven.

The brunette shook her head.

"Sweet young thing like that ain't gonna last long on these streets."

I gave her my card. "If you see or hear anything about her, give me a call. Her name is Zoe Brooks."

"You didn't hear it from me," Champagne said. "But Freddie Valentine likes them young. If anybody out here is likely to pick her up, it's him."

"You know where I can find Mr. Valentine?"

"You'll find some of his girls on Turner Street. You might be able to catch Freddie at Corner Pocket." Champaign paused. "Like I said, you didn't hear that from me."

"Thanks for the heads up."

"Just remember that next time Champagne needs a favor."

I chuckled. "I will. Thank you. You ladies be safe."

"You sure you don't want one on the house?"

I laughed. "Maybe some other time."

JD pulled away from the curb, and we continued cruising down Dowling Street to Turner. As we pulled to the curb, a young girl approached the vehicle. She was a skinny blonde with creamy skin and ocean eyes. Maybe too young. In a timid voice, she asked, "What are you looking for?"

"A girl named Zoe Brooks," I said, showing her a picture on my phone. "You recognize her?"

She shook her head.

"Are you sure?"

She studied the image again. "I'm sure. You cops?"

"She's missing. Her family is worried about her."

The girl looked around nervously. "I ain't supposed to talk to cops."

"You know it's dangerous out here. How old are you?"

"18."

"You sure about that?"

She nodded.

"You got a family somewhere?"

She shook her head. "I can't really talk anymore."

I gave her my card. "If you see or hear anything about Zoe, give me a call. If you need anything, give me a call."

She took the card and backed away from the car, glancing around to see if anyone saw her talking to us.

"You know where I can find Freddie?"

She shook her head.

I'm sure she knew, but she was too afraid to say.

It broke my heart to see these girls on the street. The lifestyle could chew you up and spit you out in a heartbeat.

We spent the rest of the day cruising around, looking for Zoe and trying to track down Freddie Valentine.

We came up empty-handed.

Isabella finally texted back. *[Cody Keller's cell phone was at Coconut Grocery from 2 PM to 10 PM the night of Austin's murder.]*

[He work there?]

[Stocker.]

I thanked her for the info. I wasn't ruling Cody out, but it seems he had an alibi.

It was the next morning when I got a call from Daniels with more grim news.

11

"We've got another extra crispy victim," Daniels said.

I groaned.

"Somebody torched another car. This time, the victim was in the trunk. I need you two to get over to that strip mall on Turnstone near Estuary Court. You know, the one with the laundromat."

"I'm on my way," I said before ending the call.

I wiped the sleep from my eyes, pulled myself out of bed, and went through an abbreviated morning routine. I grabbed my pistol and holstered it in my waistband for an appendix carry.

JD picked me up in the Porsche, and we cruised over to Turnstone. Red and blue lights flickered, and the back alley swarmed with first responders. Brenda and her crew examined the remains in the trunk while Dietrich snapped photos. The camera flashes illuminated the charred corpse. That terrible, acrid smell filled the air.

Parked near the dumpster, the car had long since burned itself out. But there was a fire truck on the scene along with EMTs, just as a matter of protocol. There was a puddle of black goo where the tires had been, and the rims sat flush against the concrete. The paint was blackened and peeling. There wasn't a stitch of fabric left in the interior.

Somehow, the responders had managed to pry the trunk open.

"Do we have an ID on the victim?" I asked as we arrived at the trunk.

Paris Delaney and crew were on the scene, grabbing footage of the charred remains from a distance.

"Not yet," Brenda said.

"The vehicle is registered to Dorothy Smith," Mendoza said. "I made a few calls but got no answer."

"This victim is male," Brenda said.

"Well, it's safe to say that's not Mrs. Smith," JD said.

"Any idea when this happened?" I asked.

"An employee discovered the car when taking trash to the dumpster this morning. He called the department. Must have happened sometime during the night." Mendoza pointed to the employee standing nearby.

He was mid 30s, slender, 6'2", with shaggy brown hair. I talked to him for a few minutes. He said he'd never seen the vehicle before, and he didn't notice it in the alley yesterday.

"Any security cameras?"

"Not in the alley. Just in the store."

"I found a wallet," Brenda exclaimed after digging around the corpse.

It was badly charred, but the positioning of the body had somewhat shielded it from the blaze. It was a sleek, metal wallet and had kept the contents well protected. Though, the plastic credit cards had melted together and fused into one giant block. The driver's license was still readable once Brenda pulled it from between the two metal plates. The elastic band that held it together crumbled away.

Brenda's eyes rounded as she read the name. "Now, this is really interesting."

She displayed the ID to me. The edges were melted, and the laminate bubbled. The whole thing was yellowed from heat, smoke, and fire. But the name was clearly readable. I knew at that moment we were dealing with something more than a robbery gone wrong.

This victim's name was Michael Williams.

Michael Anthony Williams.

Two victims with a similar name in two days. Something was fishy.

JD and I exchanged a knowing glance.

After the scene was documented, Brenda and her crew removed the remains and loaded them into the back of the medical examiner's van. Before she left, she said, "I'll pull dental records and make sure that this is who we think it is. By the way, Dr. Williams's dental records were a match."

"I'll let Megan Williams know," I said.

We wrapped up at the scene, then headed back to the station to fill out after-action reports. Afterward, we found Denise at her desk.

The office buzzed with activity. Phones rang, and keyboards clacked. The smell of stale coffee lingered in the air, and the sun filtered through the blinds. Deputies fielded complaints and processed perps.

"What can you tell me about Michael Anthony Williams?" I asked Denise.

Her manicured fingers danced across the keyboard. A moment later, Anthony's background information appeared on the screen. We all hovered around the monitor, and the delightful scent of Denise's fruity body wash filled my nostrils. It was electric.

The resemblance of Anthony's DMV picture to Austin's was striking. Same short wavy brownish-blond hair, trimmed beard, and handsome features. Anthony's face was a little narrower, and his height was listed as an inch taller. He had brown eyes as opposed to Austin's blue.

A mistaken target was sounding more reasonable.

"He's an attorney," Denise said, reading from the screen. "Married. Lives at the Trident Tower." Her emerald eyes scanned the display. "This is interesting. Questioned in the death of Erin Fisher. No charges were filed. Looks like he's had a few run-ins with the law. Busted last month for possession of cocaine. Again, no charges."

I lifted a curious brow. "Who was the arresting officer?"

"Deputy Miller. Routine traffic stop. Found a kilo of cocaine in the trunk."

"That seems like more than a personal use amount," I snarked.

"I'm beginning to think this guy was the target," JD said. "Two people killed in two days with the same name. That's a hell of a coincidence."

"I think maybe Dr. Austin Williams was in the wrong place at the wrong time," I said.

"With the wrong name," Denise added.

JD said, "Somebody hired a hitman, gave him a name, and the hitter goes out and kills the wrong guy. Talk about incompetence."

Denise's face saddened. "That's terrible. You think that's what really happened?"

I shrugged.

"Sure looks like the attorney was involved in shady activities," JD said.

Denise's fingers tapped the keys again, searching the web, looking for more information about Michael Anthony Williams. The front page of the search results was littered with juicy tidbits about the deceased. There were articles about the Erin Fisher investigation, along with several links tying Anthony to Vinnie Farina.

Denise clicked on one of the articles. We all huddled closer, reading the text. By the time we finished the piece, possible motives were plentiful.

"So, he defended Vincent Farina's son, but the kid went down for murder. Life in prison without the possibility of parole," Denise said.

"I would imagine that didn't ingratiate him to the mob," JD said.

Vinnie Farina had earned the reputation of a ruthless Mafia boss involved in everything from drugs to guns, racketeering, extortion, loansharking, and murder. But the guy was slick. Nothing ever stuck. He had charm and personality, and the media had a fascination with him. He was every bit the old-school gangster. But he was smart. He didn't have a cell phone. He didn't use email. He didn't have social media profiles. He never spoke directly about the *business*. Despite numerous investigations from multiple agencies, nobody could ever get anything on him.

"You think the mob took out the lawyer because he couldn't get Joey Farina off?" Denise asked.

"Could be," I said. "Or maybe the drug charge got them worried."

"He couldn't flip on the client. He'd be disbarred for violating the attorney-client privilege."

"He could also be disbarred for the possession of a kilo of cocaine."

"Possibly," she agreed.

Denise returned to the search page and clicked another article. After scanning it, she said, "Looks like Joey filed for an appeal, citing *ineffective assistance of counsel.*"

It was a common tactic among defendants to say that their attorney sucked and didn't provide adequate legal counsel. Still, it's hard to get away with murder when you shoot someone point-blank in a restaurant with multiple witnesses. It doesn't matter who your attorney is.

Joey Farina wasn't the sharpest tool in the shed, and he lacked the style and sophistication of his father. They say the apple doesn't fall far from the tree, but this one fell down the block.

"See what you can find out about Anthony Williams. Dig through his credit cards, bank statements, phone records. Maybe we'll get lucky and find something."

"I'm on it," she said with a smile.

I called Deputy Miller and asked him about the stop with Anthony Williams. I wanted to know why the charges got dismissed.

"The guy was speeding and weaving," Deputy Miller said when I called. "I pulled him over and smelled a significant odor of alcohol and marijuana. I had Mr. Williams exit the vehicle and asked him to perform a field sobriety exam which he declined. I searched the vehicle and found cocaine in the trunk."

"He gave you permission to search?"

Miller hesitated for a moment. "Apparently, that's the issue. Judge tossed the case."

"Who was the judge?"

"Echols."

"Figures."

"I believe I had a reasonable suspicion that drugs were in the vehicle."

"But you didn't get permission or a warrant for the trunk."

"Correct."

"Who prosecuted the case?"

"Marla Mackey. What is your interest in this anyway?"

"Anthony Williams turned up dead in the trunk of a car that belongs to a woman named Dorothy Smith."

"Well, he was a mob lawyer," Miller said dryly.

I thanked Deputy Miller for the info and ended the call.

Daniels marched across the main office with a sour look on his face and joined us. "I need you two to get over to 303 Hummingbird Lane. Mendoza stopped by Dorothy Smith's house and attempted to inform her that her car had been torched. Turns out the car is the least of her concerns."

A dreadful feeling twisted in my stomach, and the sheriff read the look on my face.

"Actually, she doesn't have any concerns at all anymore. Looks like someone waited for her to come home. Shot her twice as she entered the back door, dragged her into the laundry room, took the keys and the car."

I frowned.

JD and I hustled out of the station and met Mendoza at Dorothy Smith's residence. Brenda and the forensics team arrived shortly.

The site was despicable.

Mrs. Smith was 78 years old. She lay in a pool of blood in her laundry room. Shot in the back twice, it was clear the assailant had been waiting near the garage and had probably attacked under cover of darkness. A senseless death, all for the purpose of stealing her car to commit a few more murders.

"How long do you think she's been dead?" I asked Brenda after she had time to make a cursory examination of the remains.

"Judging by the body temperature and rate of decomposition, she's been here a couple of days. I'll know more when I get back to the lab."

"Is it safe to say she was killed before Dr. Williams?"

"I would agree with that."

"You think she was a random target?" JD asked.

"Could be," I said. "Or maybe our killer was familiar with her routine. Perhaps he knew the victim. An easy target."

"It seems sloppy for a professional hitter to kill someone he might have a connection to."

"Given the circumstances, I don't think our hitter is that professional," I suggested.

We looked through the house, and it didn't appear that anything was taken. The TV was still there. Jewelry and other valuables were in Dorothy's bedroom.

We canvassed the neighborhood, knocking on doors. No one had seen or heard anything suspicious. Two shots from a pistol in the middle of the night should have drawn the attention of the neighbors, but the killer could have used a suppressor to reduce the volume. Contrary to popular belief, suppressors do not silence a gun. They attenuate the decibels. Still, 90 or 100 decibels is fairly audible. Though muffled by the walls of a house, you might still sleep through it.

We found a neighbor a few houses down with a video door-bell. It was a long shot, but I banged on the door. The instant I did, a yappy dog went crazy, barking and growling. A woman's voice crackled through the speaker a moment later. "Who is it?"

I flashed my badge to the camera. "Deputy Wild with Coconut County. We need to speak with you for a moment."

"Is there a problem?"

I gave her the bad news. She opened the door a moment later with a tiny chihuahua cradled in her arms. The vicious guard dog snarled and growled, displaying his ferocious teeth. "Peanut, behave!"

He barked a few more times, then settled.

The woman's face crinkled with sorrow. "That's horrible. Dorothy was so sweet. Who would do such a thing?"

"We're hoping your video doorbell might have captured a glimpse of the perpetrator."

"I can certainly check the footage. Sometimes it will go off when cars pass by, but sometimes it won't."

She pulled her phone from a side pocket in her gray yoga pants. She was an attractive woman in her early 30s with sandy blonde hair. Her teal sports bra revealed a toned midriff that I couldn't help but notice. She launched the doorbell app and scrolled through the history. "Do you know when this happened?"

"We think three days ago," I said. "Probably in the late evening."

She scrolled through the footage. There were clips of pedestrians walking on the street. Kids on bicycles. Several passing cars. Nothing useful.

Then she exclaimed, "There's Dorothy's car right there!"

She handed the device to me, and I replayed the clip. Dorothy's vehicle passed by at 10:32 PM. The footage was dark and grainy. It was difficult to see and impossible to ID the driver. But the silhouette didn't fit the shape of a petite 78-year-old woman. I was pretty sure that was our killer driving away in Dorothy's car after he'd brutally murdered her. I hoped that the tech guys, or Isabella, could enhance the footage.

I asked the woman to export the clip and send it to me. "How well did you know Dorothy?"

"I saw her every day and said hello. She's lived in that house since I moved in. I've been here for five years. I think she's been in this neighborhood forever." She frowned.

"What's your name, ma'am?"

"Kristin Reynolds."

"You live here alone?"

She nodded. "Do you think this was random? I mean, I always thought this neighborhood was pretty safe."

"We think this may be connected to two other murders."

Her eyes rounded. "The doctor and the lawyer?"

I nodded.

A look of distress washed over her face.

"You know if Dorothy had any family in the area?"

"Not that I know of. Her husband passed away a few years ago. And her daughter was killed in an accident fifteen years ago. At least, that was the story I heard."

"Did she ever have any visitors?"

"Not often. She had friends that would stop by on occasion, and I think she would meet other ladies for lunch. But I never saw any family come to visit."

"Did she need any assistance?"

"She was always pretty spry for her age." Kristin sighed. "I just can't believe anybody would kill her. She was such a sweet lady. Really talented artist. She would do commissions. Pet portraits mostly. She painted one of Peanut. You want to see it?"

"If you don't mind."

"Just a minute. I'll be right back." She dashed away and returned a moment later with an 8x10 oil painting on board of her Chihuahua. It was a masterful painting. Nice brushwork, confident lines, vibrant colors. An exact reproduction of the feisty little monster.

"Beautiful work," I said as I handed the painting back to her. I gave Kristin my card and told her to call if she remembered any other details.

We said goodbye to Peanut, who finally decided to let us pet him before leaving.

Brenda and her team were finishing up by the time we returned to Dorothy's house.

We headed back to the station, filled out more reports, then drove to the *Trident Tower* to speak with Anthony Williams's wife, Alexis. Hopefully, she had additional insight. Daniels had already informed her of her husband's death.

13

The luxury high-rise towered into the sky. The attached marina was filled with yachts, sport boats, and Bluewater sailboats. There was a 24-hour concierge, valet parking, and every imaginable amenity.

JD pulled the Porsche under the carport, and the attendant handed him a ticket as he stepped out of the vehicle. Jack folded a $20 and slipped it into his palm. "Keep it up front."

"Yes sir," the kid replied with enthusiasm.

I flashed my badge at the glass door, and the concierge buzzed us in. The pretty blonde wasn't working today, but an equally eye-catching brunette greeted us with a warm smile and pearly teeth. "What can I do for you, gentlemen?"

"We're here to see Alexis Williams, #2612."

"You want me to let her know that you're here?"

"You can tell her we're on our way up."

Usually, I liked to approach suspects cold, but Daniels had already notified Alexis and told her we were on our way over. I didn't necessarily think she was involved, but you never know.

We walked across the opulent lobby, and JD pushed the call button. The elevator doors slid open a moment later, and we stepped aboard. After a few stops on the way up, we arrived at the 26th floor and stepped into the corridor. I knocked on the door to Suite #2612 and identified ourselves as police officers.

A gorgeous blonde pulled open the door a moment later. "Please, come in."

She stepped aside and motioned us into the foyer. Alexis closed the door behind us after we entered and escorted us into the living room.

It was a nice two-bedroom condo with a large, open floor plan with vaulted ceilings, floor-to-ceiling windows, and a state-of-the-art kitchen with stainless steel appliances and marble countertops. There was a second story with a loft area. It wasn't the largest unit in the building, but not a bad size and came with a healthy price tag.

We took a seat on the black leather sofa in the living room. Alexis sat across from us. Her golden hair dangled well past her shoulders, and her tan skin shimmered. She had piercing azure eyes and a mouthwatering figure. She was mid-20s, with sculpted cheekbones and plump lips. Her neck, ears, wrists, and fingers were adorned with sparkly expensive jewelry.

Alexis had definitely grown accustomed to the finer things in life.

There wasn't a wrinkle on her face. Her forehead was smooth, and her nose was perfect. I couldn't be totally sure, but she looked a little enhanced in the chest. I wondered if she knew Dr. Williams. Many of the rich socialites did.

"I'm very sorry for the loss of your husband, Mrs. Williams."

"I'm not."

Nothing stunned me anymore, but it did give me pause. "Trouble with the relationship?"

"We were in the middle of a contentious divorce. I guess that makes me a suspect, doesn't it?"

"It raises eyebrows."

"Well, I can assure you, I didn't shoot Anthony, put him into a trunk, and set him on fire. Though I have to admit, I'm slightly envious of the person who did."

"Tell us how you really feel," JD muttered.

"I feel like Anthony was a narcissistic, abusive asshole. And I'm glad I don't have to deal with him anymore. Plus, I get all his money."

"Are you trying to work your way to the top of our suspect list?" I asked.

She smiled, flashing her perfect pearly teeth. "The innocent have nothing to fear."

"Were you still living together?"

"God, no. He moved onto the sailboat. I urged him to find another marina, but he wanted to stay close by. It made it a little awkward when I brought men back to the apartment, but that's what he gets for being a dickhead."

"I see. So, you were having an affair?"

"No, Deputy, I was not having an affair. I'm randomly sleeping with whoever I want. He'd been fucking everything that walked for years. Turnabout is fair play. And no, I never once cheated on him before I told him I wanted a divorce. That's fair, isn't it?"

"At least you were upfront about it."

"Oh, I was very upfront about it," she said with glee, leaning forward, resting her elbow on her knee. "I sent him videos of all the guys I slept with since he moved out. Just to rub a little salt in the wound. And I let them do all kinds of things to me I never let him do."

"You know how to hurt a man, don't you?" JD said.

She smiled. "That, I do."

She seemed extremely proud of herself.

"Besides yourself, can you think of anyone else who may have wanted to kill your husband?" I asked.

"Everybody hates attorneys, don't they?"

"I think they draw more disdain than perhaps any other profession. What about Vinnie Farina?"

"What about him?"

"Your husband did a lot of work for Vinnie. Defended his son."

"So?"

"You're aware of Vinnie's reputation."

"I am."

"You think maybe Vinnie took retribution against Anthony for the lack of an acquittal in Joey's case?"

"Anything is possible."

"Did your husband ever talk to you about the case?"

"I didn't really want to hear about his work. I just wanted him to keep paying the bills. And clients like Vinnie had big bills."

"So you had no problem with the fact that he was defending mobsters."

"Everybody is afforded the right to adequate counsel, aren't they, Deputy?"

I nodded.

"That's how our system works."

"Have you ever met Vinnie Farina personally?" I asked.

"On a few occasions. And I found him very charming and cordial."

"Did Anthony ever mention that he was afraid of Vinnie?"

"We weren't really talking much in the last few months. Only when necessary."

"Necessary as in you sending him videos of lewd acts with other men."

"I found that very necessary."

"What about the death of Erin Fisher?"

She rolled her eyes. "She was just some stripper he was banging. Her family brought a wrongful death suit, but it was dismissed."

"You think your husband was responsible for her death?"

"No criminal charges were filed."

"That's not what I asked."

"I know what you asked, Deputy. My opinion is irrelevant. I wasn't there." She sighed. "Honestly, that was the last straw for me. I was done after that. He did receive a few death threats after the incident. There were nasty notes left on his car. The girl's brother left threatening messages on Anthony's social media profile."

"What was his name?"

"Caleb, I think."

I made a note on my phone. "Were you aware of your husband's recent arrest?"

14

---

nthony was arrested? News to me," Alexis said. "What for?"

I gave her the story.

"Doesn't surprise me."

"Was he dealing?"

She laughed. "No. For Anthony, that was a personal use amount. That's the fairy dust that keeps half the attorneys at the firm going."

"A kilo is a pretty large amount. You know where he might have gotten it from?"

Her eyes narrowed and flicked between the two of us. "Are you guys real deputies? Do you investigate real crimes?"

"Occasionally," JD muttered.

"Where do you think he got it? His clients are all degenerates. Anything he wanted was only a phone call away."

"Where were you last night between 7 and 9 PM?" I asked.

She scoffed. "Do I really look like a killer?"

She looked like she could be lethal, that was certain.

"Standard question," I said.

"Is that when he died?"

"We don't know exactly when Anthony died yet. But that's when Dr. Williams was murdered."

She lifted a curious eyebrow. "Dr. Williams?"

"I take it you haven't been keeping up with the news."

"I try to avoid the news whenever possible. Especially that bitch, Paris Delaney. That woman makes my skin crawl."

JD stifled a chuckle.

"Did you know Dr. Williams?"

"A wonderful plastic surgeon."

"With the same name as your husband."

"I never really thought about it. I always knew him as Austin."

"So, you were a client of his?"

She smirked. "I can neither confirm nor deny." Her brow knitted. "Is he really dead?"

I nodded.

"That's terrible. He really was the best. And you think these two killings are related?"

"We're looking into it."

My phone buzzed with a call from Paris Delaney. I silenced it and returned my attention to Alexis. "Well, I think we've taken up enough of your time. Again, our condolences."

"Looks like I'll be breaking out the champagne. Care to stay for a drink?"

"Thank you, but we have a murder to solve."

"Good luck, deputies."

We stood up, and she walked us to the door. She latched it behind us after we stepped into the hallway.

"She's a piece of work," JD muttered. "Think she killed him?"

"She wouldn't get her hands dirty. But I wouldn't put it past her to hire someone. She didn't try to hide her disdain for her husband."

"Maybe that's her plan. Make herself such an obvious suspect that we dismiss her."

"Time will tell, my friend. Time will tell."

I pulled my phone from my pocket to call Paris as we strolled down the hallway toward the elevator, but it buzzed before I could dial. I swiped the screen and held the device to my ear.

"Are you busy?" Paris asked.

"Not anymore."

"I just got a call I think you might be interested in."

15

"I just got an anonymous call from a guy claiming to be the shooter," Paris said. "He said Austin was a mistake, and he apologized."

"He apologized?"

"Yeah, said he felt bad about it."

"That's unusual. A hitman with a heart."

"He knew the details. Said Austin was shot twice with a 9mm. Once in the head, once in the neck. Is that correct?"

"Off the record?"

"Absolutely."

I knew nothing was ever off the record with Paris. "I mean it. Don't leak this information."

"I swear, I won't release any details discussed during this conversation."

"I think your caller could be our killer."

"You can work your magic and track the call, can't you?"

"I can try. What can you tell me about his voice?"

"He used one of those things to disguise his voice."

"Did you hear anything identifiable in the background? Sirens, music?"

"No."

"Let me know if he calls again."

"I will."

I ended the call and dialed Isabella. I filled her in on the situation and asked her to track Paris's phone. Her fingers tapped the keys, and a few moments later, she said, "The call came from a prepaid cellular. Looks like it originated from an alley near the corner of Olympic and Walnut."

"Where is the phone now?"

"Off the grid."

"Let me know if it pops up again."

"You got it."

"Thank you. You're the best."

"I know."

JD and I took the elevator down to the lobby, said goodbye to the brunette concierge, and stepped outside under the carport. The valet brought the car around, and we zipped across the island to Olympic. I had no doubt that our perp was long gone, but perhaps a security camera might have captured someone in the area using a cell phone.

The alley behind the row of storefronts where the call originated was empty.

I didn't see any surveillance cameras, and there was no one loitering around the area. We asked the store owners if they'd seen anybody lingering in the back alley, but nobody did.

"I don't know about you, but I could eat," JD said.

He wasn't going to get an argument from me.

We left Olympic and headed to Oyster Avenue. We parked at the curb and strolled the sidewalk looking for something to suit our taste buds. Tourists walked the avenue, street vendors hustled their wares, and the smell of grilled food wafted in the air. Jack wanted to try out a new fusion restaurant, *Primo Cibo*. It just opened up.

It was an upscale eatery with slate gray tiled floors, stone walls, cherrywood tables, and a sleek central bar loaded with top-shelf liquor. They had an extensive wine cellar, and the sommelier visited the table to make suggestions on the perfect complement to the meal. Of course, some of the suggested wines cost more than a four-door sedan.

I don't think the wine steward was particularly impressed with our selection of the house Pinot Noir—a light red that paired well with seafood. Though he did make a good case for the Louis Legrand Château la Régence Grand Cru. But at $250 a bottle, it seemed excessive for lunch.

JD ordered the jumbo lump crab cake topped with lemon butter for an appetizer along with fried calamari. For an entree, he ordered the Grilled Shrimp Fettuccine, and I opted for the Spicy Chipotle Seafood Risotto.

Our waitress was cute, the food was good, and the bill was somewhat reasonable. I would explore the menu again, but I think JD liked the crab cakes and calamari at *Wetsuit* better. But that could have just been the influence of the skimpy bikini bottoms and form-fitting neoprene tops unzipped down to flat midriffs.

JD paid the tab and left a fat tip. We walked back to the Porsche with full bellies, the bright sun bouncing off the sidewalk. We hopped into the car and sped across the island to *Foster, Williams, De Veen, LLP.* I wanted to speak with Anthony Williams's colleagues.

The high-powered firm took up two floors in the Westwood building. We pulled into the lot and pulled to the valet stand.

We hopped out, pushed inside, and strolled across the atrium to the elevators. It was a sleek, modern building. Well maintained. There were no fountains or Koi fish, but there were plant boxes with ferns and other greenery.

I pressed the call button, and an instant later, the bell dinged and the doors slid open.

JD's phone rang. He pulled out the device, looked at the caller ID, then swiped the screen. "Do you have the wrong number? Are you actually calling me?"

"Shut up." Scarlett's voice crackled through the tiny speaker.

JD covered the phone and whispered to me, "Go on. I'll catch up with you."

I stepped aboard the elevator and pressed the button for the fifth floor. Just as the doors slid closed, a woman shouted, "Hold the elevator!"

Her high heels clacked against the tile as I lunged a finger toward the button to hold the doors open.

She slipped inside and flashed an appreciative smile. "Thank you. Will you hit #4, please?"

I was happy to assist. She was a gorgeous brunette with wavy hair and a stunning red dress that clung to her petite form like it was vacuum sealed. She had mesmerizing green eyes, tan skin, and soft, supple endowments that I was pretty sure were all-natural—though I wouldn't mind opening an active investigation.

The doors closed, and the hydraulics lifted us skyward.

The faint traces of her perfume swirled in the air. Elegant. Understated. Not overpowering.

I had mere seconds to open a conversation. Within a few moments, we'd go our separate ways and might never see each other again. I'd be lying if I said my heartbeat wasn't slightly elevated. This woman drank up all the oxygen in the elevator and made it hard to breathe.

"Do you have any outstanding warrants?" I asked.

She lifted a curious eyebrow. "Do I look like a criminal?"

"You look like trouble."

"Trouble?"

I looked her up and down. She looked delicious. "Yeah, we would never work. So get that idea out of your head right now."

That got her attention. "Oh, really?"

"You and me together, no telling where that would lead."

"Are you a cop?"

I flashed my shiny gold badge. "Sometimes."

"So, tell me, *Mr. Deputy*," she said, her sultry eyes looking into mine. "Does this little routine always work?"

"I don't know. I've never tried it in an elevator before."

She chuckled.

"How am I doing so far?"

"I'm still talking to you, aren't I?"

"You don't really have much choice."

That's when the most fortuitous thing imaginable happened.

16

The elevator stopped abruptly, and the lights went out.

"Looks like we're stuck with each other for a little while," she said.

"I guess I'll have to suffer through it. It could be worse." I grabbed my phone and used the flashlight to illuminate the area. "Do you have any medical conditions that require urgent attention?"

She chuckled. "Not that I know of."

"You're not claustrophobic, diabetic, no heart conditions?"

"No, I'm pretty healthy. But I hope we're not trapped in here too long. Not that I don't find you amusing, but that last cup of coffee will need to go somewhere."

I pushed the call button on the elevator. It dialed a 24-hour emergency dispatch unit. The operator came on and asked for our location and confirmed that no one was in any immediate danger. She said she'd send a repair crew immediately and asked if we wanted her to stay on the line.

"That's not necessary right now," I said. "I think we have everything under control."

"I'm just a phone call away," the dispatcher said before ending the call.

"I guess I'm going to be late for my meeting," the brunette said.

"I'm sure they will understand."

She used her cellphone to make a call and explained the situation. I tried not to eavesdrop, but we were in a confined space.

"I didn't get your name," I said after she finished.

"I didn't tell you."

"Well, we are stuck in an elevator. We might as well get to know each other."

Her pretty eyes narrowed at me. "You sure you didn't have anything to do with this?"

I shrugged innocently. "Me?"

"Who knows? This could be a regular thing for you. You hit on unsuspecting young women by coordinating with the building maintenance to shut down the elevator at just the opportune time."

I chuckled. "I like to think I'm pretty well connected. But I'm not *that* well connected."

She laughed.

"And I wasn't hitting on you. You're not my type." She was totally my type.

She gave me a doubtful glance.

My phone was just about out of juice. It didn't take long for it to die completely with the flashlight on.

Suddenly we were surrounded by darkness.

"I guess I'm safe with you in the dark. You are a deputy after all."

"I can guarantee your safety."

"But what if I like a little danger?"

"An adventure seeker?"

"I like a thrill as much as the next girl." Her voice was full of possibilities.

I couldn't see a thing in the inky blackness. "Your phone has a light if you feel unsafe."

"I don't want to drain my battery?" Her voice drew closer as she took a step.

The tiny space was fully charged. Her presence was electric.

"Did you just grab my ass?" she shrieked.

"Excuse me?"

"You heard me. I distinctly felt a hand on my derriére."

"Maybe there's a ghost in this elevator."

"A likely story."

I was sure she was just messing with me, but in this day and age, you never knew.

Her presence radiated as she stepped closer. My skin tingled in the darkness. She was close now. I could feel it. She took my forearm and traced my skin with her delicate fingers down to my hand, then she pulled it around and placed it on her firm backside. Her hot breath tickled my skin. "I was right. You did grab my ass."

She clutched my shirt, lifted up on her tiptoes and planted her wet lips against mine. They were plump and soft. Her lip gloss tasted like strawberries. Her floral shampoo filled my nostrils. Her velvety tongue danced with mine, and our bodies melted into one another.

I was more than happy to continue grabbing her ass as her soft hands explored my body.

We broke for air, and an instant later, her lips were at my ear. She whispered, "I've never done it in an elevator before."

My heart pounded, and the captain stood at attention. She had a voice that could ignite a brush fire.

"You are the adventurous type, aren't you?"

"I guess I like the thrill of getting caught."

Our lips collided again, and I grabbed copious handfuls of her supple breasts. My hands glided along her rib cage and over her shapely hips. My fingers found the hemline of her dress. I slid it over her hips and cupped her smooth cheeks. Her delicate moans danced in the darkness.

My fingers slid into the waistband of her lacy panties, and soon they slid down her firm thighs and hit the floor. She stepped out of them.

Things were about to get interesting when the lights flicked on, and the elevator started in motion again.

Our lips parted. She broke away, cleared her throat, and looked at the floor meekly as she adjusted her skirt just before the elevator doors slid open on the fourth floor.

A gentleman waited in the hall to step aboard.

She smirked and stepped toward the exit. "This is my stop, Deputy."

She wiggled her fingers at me as she stepped into the hallway.

"Is it safe to get on now?" the man asked.

I shrugged, then snatched her black lace panties from the floor, pressed the button to hold the door open, and poked my head into the hall, calling after her. "I think you forgot something."

I dangled her lacy black panties.

She looked over her shoulder and smirked. "If you're a good detective, you can find me and give them back some time."

She turned the corner and continued to her appointment.

I wasn't going to chase. Never chase. I stepped back into the elevator, and the guy looked at the panties, then me. With wide eyes, he said with envy, "Lucky bastard."

I was pretty sure I could find the brunette again.

17

J D was waiting for me when I stepped off the elevator on the fifth floor. "What the hell happened?"

I shrugged innocently. "The elevator got stuck."

I showed him the pair of black lace panties that I had acquired.

His eyes rounded. "This, I gotta hear."

"Tell you later."

He frowned, not wanting to wait.

We stepped into the well-appointed lobby of the law firm—cherry wood-paneled walls with the name of the firm prominently displayed by a gold name board.

"Good afternoon, gentlemen," a woman said from behind a reception counter. "How can I help you?"

I flashed my badge. "I'd like to speak to someone about Michael Anthony Williams."

Her face crinkled into a frown. "It's so terrible. I just can't believe he's gone."

"Did you know Mr. Williams well?"

"He was a partner at the firm. I've been here for six years. I saw him every day."

"Can you think of anyone who may have wanted to do him harm?"

"I think you should talk with Mrs. Foster. She might be able to give you more insight. I just answer phones and greet people as they come in. Anthony was always kind to me. I know he liked his Grande Latte's. I know he liked to smoke cigars. Beyond that, I don't think I can tell you much."

She picked up the phone and dialed Mrs. Foster. After a brief exchange, the receptionist said, "Have a seat. Ms. Foster will be with you shortly."

We plopped down on the sofa and waited.

"So, spill it," JD whispered.

"There's not much to tell," I said, understating my elevator encounter.

"Do those belong to the brunette?"

"Could be."

JD grew green with envy.

Evelyn Foster emerged and greeted us. We made introductions, and she led us down a hallway to her office. She had shoulder-length blonde hair and wore a navy blazer and skirt. She had a face that said *don't mess with me*—years of playing hardball with tough prosecutors and good ole boys. Her blue eyes excelled at seeing through bullshit.

Her office had a nice view of the ocean through floor-to-ceiling windows. She offered us a seat across the desk from her. The furniture was sleek and modern with a minimalist design. There were framed diplomas and credentials on the walls along with pictures of Mrs. Foster and celebrity clients —athletes, musicians, gangsters.

"Your firm is mostly criminal defense, correct?" I asked.

"Mostly. But we do a little family law, and we have an attorney that specializes in intellectual property."

"But if you get in trouble, this is the firm to call, right?"

She smiled. "I like to think so."

"I suppose Vinnie Farina was pretty upset about the outcome of his son's trial."

"As any parent would be. Joey didn't get a fair shake."

"How so?"

"He got a notoriously difficult judge. The prosecuting attorney stalled on discovery, and I don't believe we got an impartial jury."

"They say a trial is won or lost during voir dire."

"Very much so. Jury selection is key."

"I understand your firm is also handling the appeal," I said.

"That is correct."

"But you're arguing ineffective assistance of counsel. You're throwing one of your own under the bus."

"I'm handling the case personally. And I will do whatever it takes for my client to prevail. I believe Joey deserves a 'not guilty' verdict."

"He shot someone in cold blood, with witnesses."

"I'm not going to discuss the specifics of the case."

"Are you more competent than Anthony Williams?"

Her eyes narrowed at me. "I have more experience. And, yes, I'm a better lawyer. I can prove Anthony was negligent in his duties."

"How so?"

"It's no secret that he was recently arrested for possession of cocaine. I can produce a number of witnesses from the office that can attest to his drug problem. His drinking problem. His questionable mental state. The added stress of his marital situation distracted him from his legal obligations. Joey Farina was not given an adequate defense. Unfortunately, this did not come to my attention until it was too late."

I surveyed her curiously. "That doesn't instill confidence in your firm."

"I'm aware of that. And I will do everything in my power to restore this firm's reputation. I told Mr. Farina I was willing to assist him in finding another attorney, but he insisted he remain with this firm. He's been a client of ours for quite some time, and he feels comfortable here."

"Even though one of your attorneys screwed up his son's defense, and the kid is now looking at life behind bars."

She forced an annoyed smile. "What can I say, Deputy? Vinnie Farina is a loyal man."

"Did he personally blame Anthony Williams?"

"I can't speak to my client's mindset."

"Does it concern you that a partner in this firm was found with two bullets in his body and burned to a crisp?"

"It concerns me greatly."

I stared at her for a moment. "Does it make you nervous to defend ruthless criminals?"

"All of my clients are innocent until proven guilty, and I resent the characterization."

"My apologies. But some of your clients do have quite the reputation."

"Reputation is not fact, Deputy. I deal in facts and only facts. You may operate on hunches and conjecture. But it's my job to present the truth and let the jury decide."

"Can you think of anyone in particular who may have had any involvement in Anthony's death?"

"I'm sure you're aware of the incident involving Erin Fisher," she said.

I nodded.

"It seems that Anthony's negligence was extending beyond his professional life and into his personal life. If I were you,

Deputy, I would seriously consider the possibility this was a revenge killing."

"We plan to speak with Caleb Fisher."

"Good. I think that's wise."

She stared at me, unflinching. She was a hard woman. She didn't break eye contact or blink, and neither did I.

"What about gambling? Did he owe anybody any money?"

"I don't know. I suppose you're also looking into his wife. He was going through a pretty nasty divorce."

"We've spoken with Alexis."

"I bet she was ecstatic."

"She wasn't upset."

I wouldn't call it a chuckle, but it was probably as close as you would ever get from Evelyn Foster.

"Do you know Alexis well?" I asked.

"Well enough to know that if I were a man, I wouldn't want to be married to her."

"Do you think she's capable of murder?"

"I don't pretend to know what someone is or isn't capable of. But I do know she is a woman that is difficult to please. She knows what she wants, and she usually gets it. From what I've seen, she has a short fuse, and I wouldn't put anything past her."

"You've seen altercations between Anthony and his wife?"

"On occasion. These spats were exacerbated by alcohol. I won't go into detail, but let's just say they had been known to make a scene or two at company functions. Quite frankly, I was relieved when Anthony told me he was getting a divorce."

"Seems like Anthony was becoming a detriment to the firm," I said.

"His behavior caused negative associations."

"He was an equity partner, correct?"

"Yes."

"Kind of hard to get rid of."

"There are provisions in place for removing a partner not living up to expectations. But, yes, it's not particularly cheap or easy."

"I guess his death saved you quite a bit of trouble," I said.

That hung there for a moment.

She didn't like it. She didn't like it one bit.

Evelyn forced a smile. "I'm afraid that's all I have time for today, gentlemen. Thank you for stopping by. You can show yourselves out."

She'd be a fool to keep talking to us. I knew as soon as I implicated any potential involvement, she'd clam up.

I thanked Evelyn for her time. We excused ourselves and said goodbye to the receptionist on the way out of the office. Despite having a good time in the elevator, we decided to take the stairs down to the lobby.

"Alright, come clean. Did you exchange fluids with the brunette?"

I thought about how to answer that. "I can tell you the flavor of her lip gloss."

"Did you seal the deal, or didn't you?"

"Give it time. This was just an appetizer."

"So, there's going to be a second encounter?"

"If I can figure out who she is," I said with a smile.

"Where is she now?"

"I don't know. She had a meeting."

"So, she could still be in the building."

"I guess that's possible."

"We could just happen to wait for her in the lobby."

"How do we know she hasn't already left?"

"Think positive."

"Trust me, I'm thinking positive. Very positive."

My phone buzzed with a call from Sheriff Daniels. My positive thoughts quickly faded. "What's up?"

"You know that missing girl? Zoe Brooks. I'm not sure she's missing anymore."

I groaned as the sensation of dread washed over me. Bad news was inbound, and I didn't want to hear any of it.

18

The sheriff's Defender class patrol boat crashed against the teal swells, spraying mists of saltwater. Sunlight glimmered the sea, and the engines howled.

We reached Barracuda Key in under an hour. Daniels piloted the boat in with the surf. We hopped out on the beach with Brenda and the forensics guys.

Two amateur treasure hunters with metal detectors and frazzled faces greeted us. One was tall and skinny, the other short and round with dark hair and brown eyes.

The short guy said, "I thought it was a coin or something small. We started to dig it up, and that's when I saw a bracelet attached to an arm bone."

"Show us," I said.

"Right this way."

They led us through the underbrush to a clearing toward the center of the island. The partially unearthed remains of a human corpse lay in a shallow grave. An earthworm slithered between the bone fragments and tattered shreds of clothing. Most of the flesh had decayed.

Dietrich snapped photos, and the camera flashes competed with the bright sun.

"Did you touch or remove anything from the grave?" I asked.

The short guy shook his head. "I thought it was a dog bone for a moment, but then I saw the hand and realized it wasn't a dog. We called you right away."

"What were you doing out here?"

"Looking for the lost treasure of Jacques De La Fontaine. It's scattered all throughout the Keys, you know."

I smirked. "I know."

"I know those kids found some on Angelfish Key, but there's more. Lots more. I've got plenty of theories."

I wasn't about to tell him of our discovery—one that we found and lost again.

Brenda snapped on a pair of nitrile gloves and hovered over the remains. She unearthed more of the figure, delicately scooping away dirt with her hands. "This is a female. Young. Late teens. But this isn't Zoe Brooks. This has been here for a while. Six months to a year, maybe. The body may have been covered with sodium hydroxide to accelerate decomposition. I'll know more when I take a closer look."

I was partially relieved that it wasn't Zoe Brooks but also concerned about who it might be.

I had a sneaking suspicion.

Brenda unearthed the skull. The teeth and jawbone were intact. If a killer is smart, they will try to damage the teeth to hinder identification. It's difficult to convict someone for murder when you haven't ID'd the victim.

I told Brenda, "Look into Sadie Bradshaw."

"The girl that went missing from Bongo Key?"

I nodded.

We'd learned of her disappearance during a previous investigation. Dean Dodd alleged that she was taken from the island by two men named Sherman and Clyde. He'd given a description of the men to a sketch artist, which I gave to Paris Delaney. Despite her broadcast and putting the sketches on the sheriff's website, no leads were generated. The sex traffickers were still at large and presumably operating their nefarious trade.

I interviewed the two treasure seekers, and they gave no reason for me to believe they had any involvement in the disposal of the remains. Neither had a criminal record. I took their names and contact information before cutting them loose.

Brenda and her crew exhumed the remains, bagged them, and loaded them onto the patrol boat. At least I didn't have to make an unpleasant phone call to Grace Brooks. Not today, at least.

Daniels took the helm, and we headed back to Coconut Key. We passed by a massive superyacht, the *Wanderlust*. JD was instantly green with envy. It was an Italian boat with sleek lines and graceful curves—especially the ones on the foredeck by the pool near the helicopter pad.

Girls in skimpy bikinis waved as we passed by, and JD waved back.

"Don't even think about an upgrade," I said.

He shrugged innocently. "I can look, can't I?"

We had all the boat we needed with the *Avventura* and then some.

We returned to the station and filled out after-action reports. I got a call from Austin's wife, Megan. "I heard a news report. Is it true that Austin's murder was a mistake?"

"It's looking that way. But we haven't been able to confirm anything yet."

She sighed. "I think that makes this whole thing worse."

She broke down into sobs, and I tried to console her. But my words weren't much help. I told her I'd keep her updated.

It was getting close to happy hour, but we decided to track down Caleb Fisher first. We caught up with him at his house on Goby Drive.

The sun plummeted toward the horizon as we pulled to the gravel shoulder in front of the chain-link fence. There were two large green trash bins out front and a row of tall palms towered along the fence line. Two American flags hung from poles attached to the trunks. We pushed through the gate and walked to the porch of the one-story sky-blue home.

I banged on the door, and a moment later a gruff voice shouted, "What do you want?"

"Coconut County!"

Caleb pulled open the door and surveyed us with suspicious eyes.

I displayed my badge.

"Like I said, what do you want?"

He looked straight out of the '70s with long brown feathered hair that hung at his shoulders. He had a mustache and a soul patch under his bottom lip, and he wore a white jersey shirt with navy blue sleeves.

"We'd like to talk to you about the death of Michael Anthony Williams."

"Couldn't happen to a nicer guy."

"You'd get along well with his wife," JD muttered.

"I imagine I would get along well with anyone who knew him."

"You made a number of threats on social media," I said.

"He killed my sister, and he walked away scot-free. What am I supposed to do? Send him good vibes and holiday cards?"

"Do you own a gun?"

"Yeah. I've got a few."

"A 9mm?"

"I've got a 9mm, a .45 ACP, a .243, a .25-06, and a 12-gauge."

"Mind if we take a look at the 9mm and run ballistics?"

He smiled. "You got a warrant?"

"No, but I can get one."

"If you could get one, you'd have gotten one. Do you think I'd be stupid enough to shoot some scumbag attorney and keep the pistol around? Do I look like an idiot?"

I refrained from making a comment.

"I heard there was another guy killed with the same name. That plastic surgeon with the billboards."

"That's correct."

"I heard somebody took credit and claimed it was a mistake. Think about it. If I set out to kill Michael Anthony Williams, I wouldn't have made a mistake."

"Maybe you did it to throw law enforcement off," I suggested.

He laughed. "Right. Look, I wasn't even in town when the doctor got killed. You need to do your homework."

"Where were you?"

19

"I was in the Bahamas," Caleb said. "Check the records."

"We will. Who did you go with?"

"My girlfriend. Want to talk to her?"

"That would be helpful."

He called his girlfriend, spoke to her for a moment, then handed the phone to me.

She confirmed his story.

I noted her name and contact information, then Caleb launched an app on his phone and showed me his electronic ticket stub from the airline. "Satisfied?"

"We'll verify the information," I said. "But I don't think we need to take up any more of your time."

He glared at us. "Nobody seemed to care this much when my sister got killed. Maybe you guys should spend more time investigating crimes perpetrated on innocent victims."

"We're very sorry for your loss."

"Sorry isn't going to bring Erin back."

He scowled at us for a moment, then slammed the door.

I could understand his frustration. Not everybody got justice. It didn't always work out. It wasn't like the TV shows. Bad guys didn't always go to jail. And sometimes, the innocent did. I didn't know if Anthony was responsible for Erin's death or not. But Caleb was right. Nothing would bring her back. Maybe Anthony's death was the Universe's way of evening the score. Karmic retribution. That was neither here nor there—I was still going to find out who was responsible and bring them to justice.

We turned around and headed back down the walkway to the Porsche. I called Denise and asked her to verify Caleb's travel. We climbed into the car, and Jack cranked up the engine. The car was on autopilot, heading to Oyster Avenue to catch the end of happy hour at *Wetsuit*. We grabbed a seat at a high-top table near the bar, chowed down on appetizers, and sipped fine whiskey.

"I say we pay a visit to the big boss himself," JD said.

"Vinnie Farina is not going to talk to us, but it's worth a shot. And I can guarantee you, if he is responsible for Anthony's murder, he didn't pull the trigger himself."

Vinnie Farina was too smart to get his hands dirty.

We chowed down, had a few drinks, then decided to change venues. *Red November* was quickly becoming one of JD's favorite hotspots. There was definitely no shortage of eye candy in the submarine-themed bar. I kept my eye out for the brunette that matched the black lace panties in my pocket. I was tempted to call Isabella and have her track the cellular data for the brunette's phone. I was pretty sure she could pinpoint another device that was in the elevator with me. But I didn't want to explain to her the reason for my inquiry, and I wanted to save my favors for when I really needed them.

Besides, there was plenty to keep us occupied at *Red November*.

It was a little after midnight when we spotted one of our suspects. JD pointed across the club at Axel. The young punk with platinum hair bought drinks for two girls. He leaned against the bar, holding court. They seemed to be succumbing to his charms. We watched him flirt for a while.

"I don't think those girls would be giggling so much if they knew Axel was a suspect in the disappearance of Zoe Brooks," JD said. "Should we spoil the party?"

"Not just yet. Perhaps we should keep tabs on our little friend."

We tried to remain inconspicuous while we watched Axel ply the young ladies with liquor for the rest of the evening. He took the two college-age blondes to a secluded booth. It wasn't long before Axel was making out with both of them.

He had the dangerous bad-boy thing going on, and the girls ate it up. They were party girls with an adventurous spirit. As the night wore on, the trio made trips to the bathroom and returned revived and alert. I never saw drugs exchange hands. But from their jittery mannerisms, and peaks and crashes, I was pretty sure they were coked up.

At 1:45 AM, the bartender shouted, "Last call."

JD settled our tab.

We lingered as the crowd thinned, then followed Axel and his girls as they spilled onto the sidewalk. They staggered amidst the sea of revelers that flooded the street at closing time.

The music had stopped, and the kitchens closed. Street vendors still hustled fajitas, tacos, and pizza by the slice to famished drunkards.

We trailed behind as Axel turned onto a side street with the girls and piled into a little red corvette parked a block away. Axel revved the engine and barked the tires as he launched from the curb. The V8 howled as he mashed the pedal and rocketed down the street, probably hitting triple digits before he turned a few blocks away.

We hustled back to the Porsche and drove to the *Coconut Club* apartments. Sure enough, we saw Axel's red Corvette in the parking lot.

"Please don't tell me we're going to sit here all night and wait for those girls to come out," JD said.

I gave him a look. "I have a plan."

20

I called Isabella and asked her to pinpoint the cell devices that were pinging the tower from Axel's apartment. She told me there were two currently on the grid, and she was pretty sure they were within his apartment. But there was always a margin of error. "One of the phones belongs to Adeline Stevens. The other, Josephine Fuller." Her fingers danced across the keyboard. "They're both students at Vanden University."

She gave me a description, as well as their ages and addresses. They lived in the Wharton Tower on campus.

"Can you give me a heads up and tell me when they are on the move?"

"I'll let you know."

Isabella sounded tired, and I don't think she appreciated being woken up in the wee hours of the morning. But she was used to it. Spies never sleep.

I figured the girls would spend the night in Axel's apartment and wouldn't surface until the morning. We went back to the marina at *Diver Down*, and JD dropped me off. I told him I'd keep him updated and hustled down the dock to the *Avventura*. The Porsche rumbled away into the night.

I settled in for the evening and didn't hear back from Isabella until after 10 AM the next morning. I had already worked out, taken Buddy for a walk, and fixed breakfast when my phone buzzed.

"Your girls are Oscar Mike," Isabella said. It was slang for *on the move*.

"Where are they headed?"

"I'll tell you when they get there," she snarked.

I grabbed my helmet and gloves and hustled down the dock to the parking lot. I straddled my sportbike and waited for Isabella to give me a destination.

"They just arrived at Waffle World."

"I owe you."

"I know."

I ended the call and slipped the phone into my pocket. No time to call JD. I cranked up the engine and revved the throttle. The exhaust note rattled with a glorious sound.

I eased out the clutch and cruised out of the parking lot. When I turned onto the road, I twisted the throttle and hugged the tank. The wind swirled around, and my heart pumped faster from an instant shot of adrenaline. I zipped across the island to the 24-hour diner, parked the bike, pulled off my helmet, and strolled inside.

A cute hostess greeted me at the stand.

I flashed my badge discreetly. "Looking for friends. Two blondes."

She pointed to a booth by the window at the far side of the restaurant near the jukebox.

I smiled and thanked her, then marched toward the girls in the blue vinyl booth. They looked a little haggard from the night before—their hair twisted and knotted, their mascara running, their lipstick smeared.

Despite it all, they still looked pretty good.

I didn't see Axel anywhere nearby. I figured the girls had taken a ride-share to the diner. The place smelled like waffles, blueberries, maple syrup, bacon, and toast. I'd already had breakfast, but it made me hungry again. Forks clinked against plates, and the subtle murmur of conversation drifted about.

I flashed my badge when I reached the booth and slid in, taking a seat beside one of the girls. They both looked at me with disdain, their faces crinkled.

"Morning, ladies. Rough night?"

"What business is it of yours?" the blonde across the table from me asked.

She was a little taller and skinnier. She had classic features and blue eyes. The girl next to me was a little shorter with brown eyes and a light dusting of freckles across her cheeks and nose. She had a little baby-fat left in her cheeks.

"I just thought you might like to know that the guy you spent the night with is a suspect in the disappearance of a high school girl."

"You're following us around?" the taller one asked in a snooty voice.

"I would hate for you girls to go missing too."

"I'm not missing. I know exactly where I am. Do you mind? I'd like to eat breakfast in peace."

"Let me guess, you're Adeline." I looked at the girl next to me. "And you're Josephine."

"How do you know our names?" Josephine asked.

I shrugged. "I'm psychic."

"Really?"

"No. Not really. You girls just happen to be involved with someone who may not be a very good person."

"Well, thank you for your concern," Adeline said. "You can go now."

"I just have a few questions for you. Do you know this girl?" I asked, displaying a picture of Zoe Brooks on my phone.

Adeline wouldn't look at it.

I showed it to Josephine.

She studied the image. "I don't know her. But I think I saw her picture on the news." Concern started to fill her eyes. "You really think Axel had something to do with her disappearance?"

"She was living in his apartment. He says she moved out, but we don't know where she went. No one has seen her since. And there's been no activity on her cell phone."

The two girls exchanged a look.

"When you were in Axel's apartment, did you see anything that might have belonged to Zoe?"

They continued to look at each other, telepathically communicating as they thought for a moment. Then they both shook their heads in unison.

"No clothes, no pictures, no personal property like a phone or a purse?"

"Not that I recall," Josephine said.

"We weren't really paying attention to the furniture," Adeline snarked.

"Did Axel offer you any drugs?"

Adeline's face crinkled. "No. We don't do drugs."

I looked at her flatly. "You're not gonna get in trouble. I just want to know if Axel's using, or perhaps dealing."

My gaze turned to Josephine, trying to pull the truth from her. She seemed the most forthcoming of the two.

She lied, "No. We just had a few drinks at the club, then went back to his place and had a few more drinks."

"According to my information, you're both 20. You're not quite old enough to be in that bar, drinking, in the first place."

Adeline rolled her eyes. "It's college. We're supposed to have fun. Don't tell me you didn't do the same thing when you were in college."

"Like I said, I'm not looking to harass you girls. I just want to find out if Axel had anything to do with Zoe's disappearance. If he didn't, I'll move on."

"When you say disappearance, you mean murder, right?" Josephine asked.

"JoJo, stop talking to this guy," Adeline snapped. Her eyes blazed into me. "I want you to leave. Now."

I ignored her. "Usually, when someone goes missing, they turn up within 48 hours. Beyond that, we start to get concerned. So, yes... I'm a little worried about Zoe Brooks. I'm concerned that maybe Axel gave her drugs. Perhaps she OD'd. Maybe he panicked and disposed of her body." I paused. "I just want to know the truth."

The girls exchanged a look.

"Did I mention Zoe was in high school and underage?"

"I don't know what to tell you, Deputy," Adeline said. "Other than I want you to leave."

"I can take a hint. I hope you girls enjoy your breakfast. You plan on seeing Axel again?" I asked as I slid out of the booth.

"That's none of your business," Adeline said. "I'll see who I want when I want."

"If you do, be careful."

I dug into my pocket, pulled out a card, and slapped it onto the table. "If there's anything you think I should know, call me. Anytime. Day or night."

Adeline grabbed the card and crumpled it up. She tossed it at me. The wadded card bounced off me and fell to the ground.

I left the girls and walked back to the hostess stand. I thanked her again before leaving, then stepped outside and called JD. "Guess who I just talked to?"

He didn't let me get a word out. "Oh yeah, well, you're not going to believe what happened to me after I dropped you off."

21

B renda beeped in on the other line before JD could start his story.

"Hang on. I gotta take this." I clicked over. "What have you got?"

"A couple things. The dental records match those of Sadie Bradshaw. Also, preliminary tests of the hair samples indicate regular heroin use."

"Cause of death?"

"It's difficult to say. There were no indications of blunt force trauma. There were no markings on the bones. She may have OD'd."

"And somebody decided to get rid of the body on Barracuda Key."

"It appears that way."

"Anything else?"

"Slugs from the doctor, the lawyer, and the old woman match."

"Not surprising." I thanked her for the update, then clicked back over to JD. I caught him up to speed. "So, let's hear about your evening."

"You're not gonna believe who called."

"That girl from the New Year's Eve show?"

"Nope. Sloan."

I tried to stifle my groan. "She called you at 3 o'clock in the morning?"

"Yep."

"I thought she was getting married."

"Apparently, the wedding is off."

I grit my teeth. This was the girl that Jack had proposed to after only three weeks. She dumped him cold, and he was lovesick for longer than the relationship had lasted.

"Please tell me she didn't come over to your house last night."

He was silent for a long moment. "I can neither confirm nor deny that."

This time I didn't stifle my frustration. "What are you thinking?"

"I wasn't the one doing the thinking, if you know what I mean."

"You can't just let her walk back in whenever she wants. She'll walk out just as easily."

"Moment of weakness."

"I'll say."

"Trust me, I'm not getting involved. I just had to console her in a moment of need. It's just what friends do."

"That girl is bad for you."

"But being bad feels so good."

"You cannot get back together with her."

"Slow your roll. Nobody said anything about getting back together. We're both older and wiser now."

"I'll give you the older part," I said dryly. "She's rebounding. You don't want to be the rebound."

"Did you ever think about the fact that her fiancé was the rebound from me, and now she's coming back to where she belongs?"

"This isn't where she belongs. And there are a few things you need to know."

"I don't know why you're getting so bent out of shape. It was just a little late-night hookup. That's all."

"I don't want to see you get hurt again."

"I'm not gonna get hurt. I'm going into this with eyes wide open."

"You're going into this with your head up your ass."

He paused, then in a suspicious tone, asked, "What do I need to know? You didn't bang her in the off-season, did you?"

"No." I hesitated. "But she came on to me one night."

He was silent for a moment. "You didn't bang her, right?"

"No. Of course not."

"Why didn't you say something?"

"I didn't want to pour salt in the wound. You'd barely gotten back on your feet."

"When?"

"That night we saw her at Tide Pool."

He took a moment to process. "That wasn't long after we split."

"That's what I'm telling you. She broke a fundamental rule. The best friend of an ex is off-limits."

He muttered again, "You didn't bang her, right?"

"I think you know me better than that."

"Just making sure." He paused. "Well, like I said. It was just a hookup."

"Hey, you're a grown man. You can do what you want. I've said my piece. I'm staying out of it. "

"At least I'm gaining valuable intel," JD said.

"How so?"

"Sloan said that Vinnie Farina is at the club every day. He plays nine holes in the morning, then has lunch in the mixed grill. Says he's terrible, but that doesn't keep him from playing."

"Doesn't keep a lot of people from playing."

"I say we go have a few words with him."

I hopped on the bike and cruised over to Jack's house. I parked in the driveway, and we transferred into the Porsche and drove to the Coconut Key Country Club. The security guard at the gate waved us through, and we drove onto the posh grounds to the valet at the main clubhouse. JD gave the attendant a nice tip. He hopped into the car and parked it up front.

We walked to the mixed grill, taking in the scenery. There were golfers practicing on the putting green. The smell of fresh-cut grass filled the air, and cleats crunched against concrete. From the mixed grill, you could watch players coming in off the 18th hole. There were ducks in a nearby pond, and you could even catch a few catfish with the skillfully placed hotdog on a hook.

I scanned the grill for Vinnie Farina, and I was surprised at what I saw.

22

———

The mafia boss sat at an outdoor table with two muscle-bound goons wearing dark sport jackets and slacks. Gold chains dangled around their necks, and I was sure there were pistols in shoulder holsters under those coats. The brunette sitting at the table with them was the surprise.

What was Elevator Girl doing with Vinnie Farina?

This would sure be an interesting time to return her black lace panties.

We approached the table, and I flashed my badge. The two goons tensed, and the brunette arched an amused eyebrow. A slight smirk curled her plump lips.

"Afternoon gentlemen, and lady," I said. "I hate to interrupt, but we'd like a few words with you about Michael Anthony Williams."

"Mr. Farina is enjoying his lunch and doesn't wish to be disturbed," a goon said.

He was a big, thick guy that filled out his suit well. He had short dark hair, brown eyes, and a chin that could take a few punches. His nose looked like it had been flattened once or twice. The goon that was sitting next to him didn't look much different. A little shorter. A little narrower in the face. A bigger nose. Hazel eyes.

Vinnie Farina was late 50s with silver hair combed to perfection. He wore a *Bandoni* suit and tie and a gold *Brivio* watch. The dapper man looked up at me and smiled as he ate. He knew we didn't have a thing on him, and he wasn't about to say a word.

The only way to make guys like that talk was to get them so pissed off they couldn't hold their tongue. But Vinnie Farina wasn't the kind of guy you wanted mad at you.

"Seems like he did a poor job with your son's defense," I said. "I would imagine he wasn't one of your favorite people."

"You're disturbing Mr. Farina," the big goon said.

"So, how do you all know each other?" I asked. "I assume you two are *security* for Mr. Farina." My eyes flicked to the brunette. "But you, I can't quite figure out."

"Don't say a word to him, Gia," the big goon said.

"Gia," I echoed in an amused tone.

The goon grimaced at his slip.

"That's a pretty name," I said.

"Thank you," she replied.

The big goon scowled at me. "Mr. Farina would like you to leave now."

"Is he unable to speak for himself?" I looked right at Vinnie. "Do you always let these guys boss you around like that?"

Vinnie maintained his pleasant demeanor, but his eyes weren't smiling any longer.

The big goon stood up and squared off against me.

"This is a private club. Members only. Go before I have you escorted out."

I smiled at the thug. "Funny thing is, I'm a member, too. And I just love meeting new members. I'm Deputy Tyson Wild, and this is my partner Jack Donovan. Pleased to meet you," I said, extending my hand.

He didn't take it.

We stared at each other for a long, awkward moment.

I flashed an annoying smile. "Well, enjoy the rest of your lunch."

We looked around for a nearby table and took a seat just to annoy Vinnie and company. I ordered a cheeseburger, and JD got a turkey club sandwich.

Vinnie and his entourage finished their meal and left.

"I hope we didn't run you off," I shouted after them with a mouthful.

Vinnie and his goons ignored us.

I watched the brunette's sultry hips sway. Her high heels clacked against the concrete as she strutted away. She gave a last glance over her shoulder and wiggled her fingers goodbye as she left the patio area.

"Do you know her?" JD asked.

"That's Elevator Girl," I said with a cocky grin.

His eyes rounded. "Little black panties?"

I nodded.

"You sure do know how to pick them."

"I didn't know who she was," I said innocently. "Still don't."

"You think that's his wife, mistress, or daughter?"

"Shouldn't be hard to find out."

23

I called Isabella. "What can you tell me about Vinnie Farina?"

"What do you want to know? The guy's pretty notorious. Seemingly untouchable."

"Tell me about his goons, his wife and kids, and any action he might have on the side."

Her fingers danced across the keyboard. "His wife's name is Marguerite. I'm sure you're familiar with his son, Joey. He's got a daughter named Gia."

"That's what I wanted to know. Thank you."

Her fingers tapped the keys again. "Oooh, she's cute. Don't tell me you're—"

"No. Just professional curiosity."

"Right," she said, knowing better. "Watch yourself."

"Always," I said.

"I'll text you info on his crew."

"Thank you."

We finished lunch and watched golfers putt out on the 18th. It was a beautiful day. Perfect for chasing the little white ball around green fairways. The smell of the mixed grill wafted through the air, and stuffy country club types dined and gossiped.

Denise buzzed my phone. "A woman just called the department looking for you."

"Oh really? Who?"

"Said her name was Gia. I'm not in the habit of giving out your personal phone number, but I told her I would pass along her information."

"Well, that is interesting."

"Who is she?"

"Vinnie Farina's daughter."

"Why is she calling you?"

"Maybe it's my charming personality."

"Good Lord, Tyson, she's a suspect in a murder investigation."

"She is not a suspect. Her father is. And she could provide valuable intel."

"I'm sure your interest is strictly limited to intelligence gathering."

"Don't worry, she's totally not my type."

"Nice try. I pulled her DMV photo. She's gorgeous."

"Okay, she's not hideous. I'll give you that."

"I'll text you her number. You better watch yourself with this one."

"She seems harmless," I said, trying to downplay it. "Oh, by the way, I have a mission for you, should you choose to accept it."

"What kind of mission?"

"You're always looking to get out of the office and be more involved."

"You have my attention."

"It's simple. You just have to dress cute, go to the bar where Axel Everhart works, and see if you can buy cocaine from him."

"I can do that. Why?"

"Because he knows more about Zoe Brooks than he's saying, and we need leverage."

"I'm game. When do you want to do it?"

"Let's see if he's working tonight."

"I'll call the bar and find out if he's on the schedule." She hesitated. "Should we clear this with Daniels?"

"Probably."

"I'll work on that and report back."

She ended the call, and a few minutes later, my phone buzzed with a text containing Gia's contact info.

I grinned and showed it to Jack.

"I wonder what she wants."

"Let's find out." I dialed the number, and Gia picked up after a few rings.

"Hello?"

"Did you enjoy your lunch at the country club?" I asked.

"I see you got my message at the Department."

"I did. You never told me you were Vinnie Farina's daughter."

"You never asked."

"You always go around seducing deputies in elevators?"

She laughed. "Not usually, but I could be tempted to do it again."

"Just let me know when and where."

"It doesn't have to be on an elevator. I'm sure we could meet somewhere equally stimulating."

"Well, I guess we'll have to see each other again sometime if you want your panties back."

A passing waitress caught my last statement and gave a shocked look before moving on.

"You're not afraid of my father?"

"I'm not afraid of anybody."

"Most guys are a little wary. I don't think he'd like it very much if I got involved with a cop."

"I'm sure you've done plenty of things your father wouldn't approve of."

"I'm not sure how to take that. Are you saying I'm a bad girl?"

"I seem to like bad girls."

"You know what they say—opposites attract. I take it you're a good cop?"

"I like to think so."

"One of those. Truth, justice, and the American way, right?"

"Something like that."

"Do you seriously consider my father a suspect in the death of Anthony Williams?"

"He has a motive."

Gia scoffed. "Because Williams lost a case, you think my father had him whacked?"

"Not just any case. Joey's case. I'm keeping my mind open to all possibilities."

"You watch too much TV, Deputy. My father is nothing like you perceive him to be."

"You just said most men are afraid of him. He's not a high-level Mafia boss involved in racketeering, extortion, drugs, loansharking, and murder?"

She chuckled. "My father is an upstanding member of the community. He's a successful real estate developer. He owns a chain of convenience stores and is one of the largest contributors to the food bank. He's a major supporter of the local fire department, and he makes generous donations to the mayor's campaign."

"All that may be true, but you can't deny your father has quite the reputation."

"Gossip and rumor are not facts, Deputy. You deal in facts, don't you?"

"I do."

"And despite numerous investigations, has anyone ever produced a shred of evidence that my father is involved in illegal activity?"

I didn't say anything.

"Didn't think so."

"Well, I'm going to continue my investigation until I am thoroughly satisfied he did not have a hand in Anthony Williams's death."

"I support your dedication and wish you nothing but the best in pursuing the truth. I just hope you are able to remain objective."

"Of course."

She paused. "It was nice to see you again this afternoon."

"You as well."

"I'll be in touch. Perhaps we can schedule a time for you to return my panties."

The way she said the word sent a charge through my ear and straight down to my pelvis.

"Perhaps we can make a trade," she said.

"What kind of trade?" I asked.

24

"You can exchange them for another pair of my panties."

I swallowed hard. I wouldn't mind seeing her entire collection. Delightful visions danced in my head of frilly, lacy things in a variety of colors—black, red, white, pink. Half the fun was taking them off.

"Enjoy the rest of your day, Deputy," Gia said. "Good luck chasing bad guys."

I ended the call and needed a cold shower.

"Playing with fire," JD cautioned. Like he was one to talk.

We left the mixed grill and bumped into Sloan as she was exiting the pro shop.

She looked good in that tight little golf skirt. Sloan was breathtaking. Funny, smart, sexy. It would take a hell of a lot of willpower to say *no* to her at 3 AM. I couldn't fault Jack too much for his moment of weakness.

"Jack, what are you doing here?" she asked, surprised.

"Just a bit of business."

"Tyson, it's good to see you again," she said in a more formal tone.

There was an awkward moment between the two of them. Neither really knowing how to behave in public toward one another.

"Getting a little practice in?" JD asked.

"Gotta stay on top of my game."

As a pro golfer, Sloan was on the lynx 24/7. If she wasn't off playing in a tournament somewhere, she was striking the ball down the green fairways of the country club.

A guy emerged from the pro shop a moment later and put his hand affectionately on Sloan's back. "You ready?"

He looked curiously at the two of us.

Sloan swallowed hard and shifted uncomfortably. "Honey, have you met Deputies Donovan and Wild?"

The man smiled and extended his hand.

"This is my fiancé, Christian Hutton."

JD had no choice but to shake the man's hand. He put on a good smile, but his eyes burned into the guy.

Christian Hutton looked like he belonged on the cover of a men's fashion magazine. He was early 40s with perfect teeth, a square jaw, ice-blue eyes, and short dark hair. He was 6'1", fit, and athletic with a leisurely tan. And he had more money than he knew what to do with. His superyacht was docked at the club marina.

"It's nice to meet you both," Christian said. His attention turned back to Sloan. "We better get going."

"Good to see you," Sloan said as Christian ushered her to a nearby golf cart. The two hopped aboard, and Christian put the cart into gear and hit the accelerator. The electric motor whined as the cart zipped down the path.

Jack's jaw was tight, and his cheeks red.

"I told you she was bad news."

"She didn't have a fiancé last night."

"Deep breath," I said.

A furious scowl twisted his face. He filled his lungs, held it for a moment, then released a slow exhale. "I'm good. I'm over it. It doesn't bother me."

He glared at the couple as they hopped out of the cart and approached the first tee. Sloan gave a guilty glance in our direction. Then she bent over gracefully, drove her tee into the ground, and placed the little white Spawn of Satan on top of it. She lined up her clubhead, planted her stance, and wiggled her booty. Focus filled her eyes, and she slowly drew the club head back.

WHACK!

The metal driver pinged, and the little white ball took flight. I lost sight of it in the bright blue sky.

JD grumbled under his breath as we marched toward the parking lot. "That woman has some explaining to do."

"Run away, dude. It's the only safe play."

We hopped into the Porsche, and JD took out his aggression behind the wheel, launching out of the parking lot and driving like a bat out of hell back to his house. I picked up my bike and followed JD to *Diver Down*. We stopped in at the bar and talked to Teagan. It wasn't anywhere close to happy hour, but that didn't stop JD from putting back a few whiskeys. I listened to him bitch and moan until he got it out of his system.

Denise called to tell me that Axel was scheduled to go on shift at 7 PM at the *Helm Station*. We made plans for our sting operation and picked her up from her apartment at 8:30 PM.

Jack waited in the parking lot while I dashed up to her unit. I had heart palpitations when she pulled open the door. If I went into cardiac arrest, I wouldn't mind her giving me a little mouth-to-mouth.

Denise wore this little black V-neck dress that showed off the girls and offered gratuitous views from the side. It cut in around her midsection, and a skimpy piece of fabric covered her hips. The hemline hung just below the promised land and displayed her shapely thighs. She wore stiletto heels that accentuated her toned calves. Her creamy skin and sparkling emerald eyes were jaw-dropping. This was a far cry from her polyester duty uniform.

"How do I look?"

She knew damn good and well how she looked. It took me a moment to formulate a coherent sentence. "You look captivating."

She smirked. "That's the point, isn't it?"

"I have something for you." I pulled out a jewelry box and opened the lid. An emerald necklace sparkled.

"For moi?" she asked modestly with her hand to her heart.

"Don't get too excited. It's not real."

She frowned adorably.

"Spin around."

She did, and I placed the necklace, dangling around her elegant collarbones, and latched it. The open back of her dress drew my eye all the way down her spine. She had a nice backside.

She turned around, and the fake jewels sparkled.

"There's a camera and a mic in the gemstone."

"Fun!"

The camera was full HD and wireless. I could watch the footage from an app on my phone. The battery would last about 24 hours.

"If he's dealing, I have no doubt you'll be able to work your magic."

A sly grin tugged her inviting lips. "Trust me. I can make him do dumb things."

"I don't doubt that."

She could make any man do dumb things.

She locked her apartment, and I escorted her to the parking lot. I opened the door for her and let her climb into the back seat. There was no way I could fit back there.

We zipped to Oyster Avenue with the top down and the night air swirling. We found a place to park and prepared for the mission.

JD pulled his hair into a ponytail and put on a hat. I pulled on a ball cap as well, then launched the video app on my phone to make sure the camera in Denise's necklace was working.

"Radio check, over," Denise said.

Both the audio and video transmitted to my phone flawlessly.

"We're good to go," I said.

The three of us made our way down the sidewalk, weaving through the tourists and revelers. The glow from signage bathed the street, and the air was alive with anticipation. The night was full of possibilities. For most on the strip, it hadn't yet been soured by alcohol and bad decisions.

The *Helm Station* was a casual bar that was styled to look like the bridge of a ship. There were life preservers on the walls and fake portholes.

We slipped into a booth near the entrance and tried to remain inconspicuous while Denise sauntered to the main bar. She took a seat on a stool and ordered a drink from our target.

The show was about to start.

25

A woman like Denise, alone in a bar, wearing that dress, wouldn't be alone for long. Almost instantly, the sharks began to circle. One by one, overly confident men approached. Some good-looking, some not so much.

The interaction was almost always the same.

"Can I buy you a drink?"

Denise would smile and say, "No thank you. I'm waiting on a friend."

"I could be your friend."

"I'm sure you could. Do you want to be friends with my boyfriend too?"

Most of them ran away with their tails between their legs. Some of them got rude. None of them had anything the least bit interesting to say. Most guys have the lamest approaches. Pretty young girls get hit on multiple times a day. Their default answer is always *no* unless you are intriguing enough to break through the shield.

"Your guy must be pretty special," Axel said.

"What makes you say that?" Denise responded.

"He's making you wait, and it seems like you've got plenty of options."

Denise smirked.

"I can tell you one thing, I would never make you wait."

I rolled my eyes.

Denise leaned in and whispered, "Don't tell anybody, but I'm not waiting on my boyfriend."

That was exactly what Axel wanted to hear. He puffed up, and a glint of opportunity flickered in his eyes. "Who are you waiting on?"

"My dealer. And he better get here soon!"

I worried she might have been a little too obvious about it, but apparently, Axel was thinking with the little brain. Easy to do around Denise. "Well, if he doesn't show, I might be able to point you in the right direction."

Denise lifted an intrigued eyebrow. "Really?"

"What exactly are you looking for?"

"I like to powder my nose every now and then."

Axel chuckled. "I might be able to help you out. And I can guarantee the quality."

Axel was on the hook. Denise just needed to reel him in.

But that's when things went downhill.

"Oh my God, what are you doing here!?" Hannah slurred as she approached. The gorgeous blonde was well into her cups. Her bleary eyes looked Denise up and down, taking in her exquisite form. "Look at you. What are you all dolled up for? Hot date?"

Hannah was a knockout that liked to party. A little too much.

"I'm meeting someone," Denise said, giving her the eye.

Hannah grew intrigued, oblivious. "Oooh, who is he? Do I know him? Have I met him before? Is it that hot deputy friend of yours?"

Axel observed the interaction with curiosity.

"No. I'm meeting someone else."

"Now I'm really intrigued."

"I take it this isn't your connection," Axel said.

Hannah's eyes narrowed at him, confused. "Connection?"

Denise elbowed Hannah. A wave of realization washed over the blonde's face. "Oh, you're undercover. How exciting!"

I clenched my jaw, and my fists tightened.

"What are you talking about?" Denise said, trying to salvage the situation.

"Oh, right." Hannah winked exaggeratedly. "Gotta keep it on the down-low. My bad."

Hannah zipped her lips with a motion. She leaned against the bar and said to Axel, "Isn't my friend the hottest deputy you've ever seen in your life?"

"Yeah, she's pretty hot for a cop."

Axel moved to the other end of the bar.

Denise muttered to Hannah, "Thanks. You totally blew my cover."

"Did I? I'm sorry. I feel terrible. Who were you trying to bust."

"Let's not talk about this here."

Hannah gave her a drunken, sloppy hug. "I'm sorry. You forgive me, don't you?"

I could almost smell the whiskey on her breath from here, and I was across the room.

"I forgive you," Denise said. "But I got all dolled up for nothing."

"Girl, the night is young. And looking like that, you can certainly get *undercover* with somebody."

Denise put a wad of cash under her glass and left the counter with Hannah. They sauntered across the club.

I shook my head discreetly at Denise when she made eye contact. I didn't want Axel to connect her with us.

Denise asked Hannah, "Who are you here with?"

"I was with Katie, but I don't know where she went?" Hannah glanced around the club, unable to spot her friend. "I think she left with some guy."

"How much have you had to drink?"

"A lot."

"Come on. Let's get you home."

Hannah's face crinkled. "I don't want to go home. I don't turn into a pumpkin until sunrise."

Hannah couldn't walk in a straight line.

"Looks like I'm babysitting for the rest of the evening," Denise said, directing her comment into the mic.

"I don't need a babysitter," Hannah protested.

"Then let's grab something to eat. Sober you up a bit."

"I paid good money for this buzz. I'm going to enjoy it."

Denise had her hands full. She wasn't going to leave her friend alone in that condition.

Just as Denise had convinced Hannah to make a venue change, Katie walked in through the main doors.

Hannah's eyes rounded. "Oh my God, where have you been!?"

A mischievous smirk tugged Katie's lips. She shrugged innocently. "I don't know."

"What do you mean *you don't know*? Where's what's-his-name?"

She shrugged again.

Hannah's eyes narrowed at her. "Did you bang him in the parking lot?"

"I can neither confirm nor deny."

"Slut."

Katie laughed.

"Can you make sure she gets home okay?" Denise asked Katie.

"Yeah, sure. You look hot. What are you doing?"

"She's undercover," Hannah whispered.

Katie looked Denise up and down. "Looking like that?"

"She's looking for drugs," Hannah whispered again.

"Honey, you ought to be able to find just about anything you want in that dress," Katie said. "Want to do a shot?"

Denise smiled. "No, thank you."

"Shot time," Hannah slurred. She grabbed Katie's arm and pulled her toward the bar. "Bye, Denise. Sorry."

JD and I slipped out of the booth and met Denise outside. She had a sad puppy dog look on her face. "Sorry, guys. I didn't expect to run into anybody I knew."

"Your friend is a handful," JD said.

"Yes, she is." Denise sighed. "Now what?"

"Plan B," I said.

"What's plan B?"

"I don't know. I'll tell you when I figure it out."

"Since that was a bust, I might as well put this outfit to good use. Let's go to Keys."

She wouldn't get an argument from me. Keys was an upscale piano bar with smooth jazz music, pretty people, and expensive drinks.

JD and I were a little underdressed for the venue, but nobody was going to turn us down with Denise in tow. We stepped inside and found a table not far from the piano. There was a good crowd. A woman in a tight red strapless evening gown had a voice like velvet, and the man behind the keys tickled the ivories with soul. The waitress served us a round of drinks, and we all clinked glasses.

"At least we tried, gentlemen," Denise said.

Having your cover blown in the wrong situation could be deadly. So, all things considered, this was just a minor inconvenience.

We were in the middle of our second round when I saw Marla Mackey enter with a companion. They made their way to the bar and leaned against the counter.

As the prosecutor that let Anthony Williams walk on drug charges, I wanted to have a few words with her.

26

"The case wasn't strong enough," Marla said. "It's as simple as that. There is no grand conspiracy."

Marla had short blonde hair with a boyish cut. She had a hard, square face with no-nonsense blue eyes. The courtroom had added a few wrinkles. She was used to going up against tough defense attorneys and stubborn old judges.

"Deputy Miller had no probable cause to search the trunk. I could have taken it to trial, but the state would have lost. That would cost the taxpayers money."

"You didn't cut him a deal?"

"There was no deal to cut."

"I just find it odd that a defense attorney for one of the most notorious gangsters in the area walked on a possession charge."

"What are you suggesting?"

I shrugged. "I'm not suggesting anything. It seems Anthony Williams was a competent attorney up until the point that he wasn't."

"As you know, drugs and alcohol can addle the mind. Perhaps he lost focus, and that's why he lost the Joey Farina case."

"It was pretty open and shut, wasn't it?"

"Nothing is open and shut when it comes to the Farinas."

"What do you mean?"

"You seem like a smart guy, Deputy. They hire the best defense money can buy and typically spare no expense when it comes to legal matters. Witnesses and jury members are often... how can I put this delicately? Intimidated."

"Are we talking jury tampering and obstruction of justice?"

"Like I said, you catch on quick."

"So what went wrong in Joey's case?"

Marla shrugged. "I don't know. Maybe the jury had principles. Maybe the witnesses weren't scared and couldn't be intimidated."

My eyes narrowed as I surveyed her. "Or maybe you had an arrangement with Mr. Williams."

She lifted an offended eyebrow. "That's a bold allegation, Deputy."

"It must be frustrating to watch criminals get off because they can bribe and threaten jurors and witnesses."

"It is, but that's the way the world works. Life's not fair. Justice is merely an idea. Something we aspire to. We don't always achieve it."

"Do you think Vinnie had Anthony killed?"

She shrugged. "I don't know. Bring me evidence, and I'll try to make it stick." She paused. "Now, if you'll excuse me, Deputy. I like to leave the office at the office."

"Sorry for interrupting."

I left her at the bar.

Denise and JD looked at me with curiosity as I approached the table and took a seat.

"She didn't look too thrilled to talk to you," JD said.

"I don't think she was." I caught them up to speed.

"You really think Anthony Williams threw Joey's case?" Denise asked.

"If it saved him from jail time and getting disbarred, maybe he just didn't fully apply himself. Maybe his negligence was intentional."

"If Vinnie found out about an arrangement between the two, that would certainly be a motive," JD added.

We stayed at *Keys* for a few more drinks and kicked around multiple theories. But that's all they were. We decided to call it a night, left the bar, found the Porsche, and drove Denise back to her apartment. JD pulled into the visitor parking lot and drove up to the main entrance.

I hopped out, pulled the seat forward, and offered the smoldering redhead a hand. Her luscious legs slipped out of the vehicle, and I pulled her to her feet.

Her face crinkled with disappointment. "Sorry about tonight, guys."

"No worries," I said. "You win some. You lose some."

"Good night, JD," she said.

"Good night, sweetie."

"I'll walk you up," I said.

"Oh, no, you won't."

I raised my hands innocently. "I just want to make sure you get in safe."

"I'll be just fine." She waved her little clutch. "I'm packing my little friend."

Denise could take care of herself, and she was pretty handy with a pistol. She lifted on her tiptoes and gave me a peck on the cheek. She pushed me away before I got any funny ideas.

"What's the matter?" I asked. "Don't you trust yourself alone with me?"

"Not in this dress, and not after that many drinks."

I smirked.

"And I'm not going down that road with you."

"What road?"

"Good night, Tyson."

"Good night, Denise."

She spun around and sauntered toward the lobby, her heels clacking against the sidewalk. Her hips swayed in hypnotic ways. She knew we were both watching, transfixed by her assets. She looked back over her shoulder with a diabolical grin on her face and waved as she pushed into the lobby.

I watched until she got on the elevator, then I hopped back into the vehicle and tried to stop thinking about her.

"Damn, son," JD muttered.

"I hear you."

"One of these days, she's going to get away. Then what are you going to do?"

I didn't have a good answer.

JD pulled out of the parking lot, and we zipped across the island to *Diver Down*. He drove around to the dock and dropped me off. I said I'd catch up with him in the morning, then hustled to the *Avventura*.

The moon hung bright in the sky, and the stars flickered. Waves lapped against hulls, and the boats gently swayed. There was a cool night breeze coming off the water. I had a visitor waiting for me on the aft deck. I crossed the passerelle and greeted Gia with a curious grin.

"Are you stalking me now?"

"I decided I wanted my panties back. They were expensive."

"Did you bring something to trade for them?" I asked.

"Sadly, I'm not wearing any panties right now. You think we can still work something out?"

27

It would be rude not to invite her in for a drink. I was investigating her father. Not her.

She knelt down and loved on Buddy. The little Jack Russell soaked up the attention.

Who wouldn't?

I rounded the bar and poured two glasses of amber liquid. We lifted our glasses to toast.

"To meeting strangers in elevators," she said, her voice full of possibilities.

I sipped the whiskey, and it heated my tongue. Her sultry gazed stoked fires of their own.

It wasn't long before we picked up where we left off. Like a magnet, her lips drew me close. I tasted her sweet lipgloss and the remains of whiskey on her tongue. My hands traced the graceful curves of her body.

They were inspiring to say the least.

With the gentle tug of my fingers, her skirt was over her hips, and my hands explored her smooth derriére. I can confirm that she had, indeed, gone commando. There were no frilly garments to impede my exploration of her sublime valley.

Our mouths merged, and our tongues danced. Her steamy moans filled my ears, and I breathed in her sweet scent. Heat radiated from her body as I pulled her close. Desire burned like a hot coal.

I kneaded her fleshy mounds and perky peaks.

Gia fumbled with my waistband, and soon there was nothing between us. She dropped to her knees and saluted the captain. She knew how to give a salute.

Fluffy watched the whole thing from the settee, unimpressed.

I pointed toward the forward cabin. But Buddy just watched. Finally, Fluffy left, and Buddy chased after the prissy white cat.

Gia and I stumbled toward the sofa and toppled to the cushions. Our hips collided, and our bodies melted into one another. Her screams filled the salon, and her manicured nails clawed my back. My heart punched my chest.

She wrapped her legs tight around me. We tried to break the sofa and definitely put it through its paces. I don't think this was covered under warranty.

I lost track of time as we entered another dimension. Slick with sweat and pulses pounding, we reached an operatic crescendo.

Tension and release.

Out of breath and exhausted, I collapsed beside her, my brain swirling with a mix of whiskey and pleasure chemicals. My skin tingled, and the whole world seemed to buzz on a sub-perceptual frequency—one that only we could feel. I didn't care if she was a mob boss's daughter. She was a damn good time.

We hit a few more locations before retiring to my master stateroom on the bridge deck for the final round. Afterward, she curled up beside me, a smooth leg draped across mine. Her delicate fingers stroked my chest.

I passed out in a state of bliss.

When I woke in the morning, the sheets were empty. My hand felt around the mattress, but I didn't discover a warm body.

I peeled open a sleepy eye. Sunlight sliced through the cracks in the blinds, painting streaks of light across the deck.

"Gia?" I called out.

There was no response.

I pulled myself out of bed and looked in the en suite.

She wasn't there.

I staggered down to the salon. Her skimpy dress was no longer on the deck. No sign of her stilettos.

I called for her again, but there was no reply. She had snuck out in the middle of the night, and I can't say I was too surprised. She struck me as a free spirit. She did what she wanted when she wanted. Not the type of woman to be tied down or answer to anyone.

I staggered into the galley like a zombie. There was a sticky note on the refrigerator. *Thanks, Deputy. I had fun. Maybe next time I'll wear panties. Or maybe I won't.*

She drew little hearts and signed the note with a fancy G.

I put on a pot of coffee, fixed a ham and cheese omelette, bacon, and hash browns. I had worked up an appetite.

I crunched on the crispy bacon, sipped my coffee, and enjoyed the omelette in the breakfast nook. As I was finishing up, there was a knock on the salon door.

I ambled into the salon and saw Vinnie's two goons standing on the aft deck, wearing gray suits, black dress shirts, and dark sunglasses.

The morning light cast amber rays across the marina.

I didn't have my pistol handy, but if these guys were here to start trouble, they would have started it already. I slid open the glass door and greeted them with a forced smile. "Good morning, gentlemen. What can I do for you?"

28

"Have a good time last night?" the big goon asked.

"I always have a good time." My eyes darted between the two of them. "You are Dino," I said, pointing to the bigger one. "And you're Enzo."

"Good for you," Dino said. "You've done your homework."

"It's part of the job."

"So you're smart enough to know what I'm going to tell you next."

"I can figure it out."

"That's good. That'll save us both a lot of trouble."

"You want me to stay away from Gia."

Dino shared a faux impressed look with Enzo. "See, I knew he was smart."

"Gia's an adult," I said. "She can make her own decisions."

Dino's smile faded. "Trust me, pal. You don't want to go down this road."

"That's my line."

"This is a whole new world you're playing in."

"Not really. I'm kinda used to dealing with guys like you. Newsflash, it never really works out well for your type."

The muscles in Dino's jaw flexed. "So, you're one of those. A little too cocky for your own good. Keep it up and let me know how that works out for you."

"Are you threatening a law enforcement officer?"

"Not at all. What would give you that impression?"

I shrugged. "Oh, I don't know. The fact that you show up at my boat in the morning and tell me to stay away from Gia."

Dino shrugged it off. "No, you misunderstand," he said in a slow gentle voice. "I'm just looking out for your best interest. She's not a girl you want to get involved with."

"What kind of girl is she?"

He smiled again, then looked me dead in the eyes. "One that you don't want to get involved with."

I chuckled. "Well, thanks for stopping by, gentlemen. I'll take your advice into consideration."

"You should do more than that. I would hate to see you get heartbroken. She's nothing but trouble. A real man-eater."

I couldn't contain my laughter. "I'm so touched you would express such concern over my emotional health."

Dino shrugged and lifted his hands. "I'm just a thoughtful, sensitive guy, looking out for my fellow man."

"Your compassion is duly noted."

We stared at each other for a long moment.

"Have a nice day, Deputy."

He tapped Enzo's arm and nodded toward the passerelle. The two spun around and marched away. Dino definitely gave the orders, which I assumed came directly from Vinnie.

I wasn't getting involved with Gia just to get under Vinnie's skin. But if it irritated him, all the better. At least, that's how I felt at the time.

Denise called. "Hey, I may have redeemed myself from last night's abysmal failure."

"How so?"

"I was able to pull credit card records for Anthony Williams. His last charge was at Forbidden Fruit. And get this. It was two days before Austin's murder."

I lifted an intrigued eyebrow. "Maybe he just didn't use the card in the interim," I said, playing devil's advocate.

"Well, I'm sure you boys will have fun investigating. Guess what kind of car Anthony drove."

"Don't say a Porsche."

"A red 911 convertible, just like Austin Williams."

"Interesting." I could see how Austin could easily have been mistaken for Anthony or vice versa.

I thanked Denise, then dialed JD and caught him up to speed. He swung by the marina and picked me up shortly thereafter. I hopped into the Porsche and pulled the door shut. He zipped away as I buckled my safety belt, music pumping through the Bose speakers. "You're not going to believe what happened to me last night."

"After I dropped you off?"

I had a shit-eating grin on my face as I nodded.

"Did you go back over to Denise's apartment?"

"No. I had a visitor."

His eyes filled with curiosity.

29

Forbidden *Fruit* was the premier adult establishment on the island. A place we were no strangers to. At this time of day, it wasn't very crowded, but they did good business with the lunch buffet.

We pulled into the parking lot behind the establishment and it didn't take me long to spot Anthony's car—a red Porsche 911 convertible. The plates matched.

JD pulled into a parking space. We hopped out and surveyed the area.

"Something tells me Anthony never made it home from the club," JD muttered as we looked around the vehicle.

I found a 9mm shell casing that had been flattened by traffic. It had been more than a few days, but I found what looked like crusted blood spattered on the asphalt, dried and brown.

"He leaves the club, goes to his car," JD theorized. "Shooter pulls into the parking lot, shoots him, stuffs him into the trunk, and drives off."

Sounded reasonable.

I glanced around but didn't see any security cameras in the parking lot.

"You'd think somebody would have seen or heard something," JD said.

"It's loud inside the club. If our shooter used a suppressor and shot from within a vehicle, the incident could have gone unnoticed."

I called the forensics team, and we waited for them to arrive. They collected the shell casing and took blood samples from the asphalt.

We walked to the front of the building and pushed in through the main entrance. The cashier waved us in. We were familiar faces.

Pop music thumped through massive speakers. Girls in high heels slinked around chrome poles. Spotlights slashed the hazy air. Toned bodies writhed and undulated, stoking lewd fantasies. Entertainers in various states of undress stimulated clients with private dances.

We found Jacko at the bar, and he greeted us with a smile and a handshake. "Who died this time?"

Jacko was tall, with slick dark hair, a sharkskin suit, and a gold chain around his neck. Jacko looked the part, but he was a nice guy, and he always treated us well. He was straight up. No BS.

158 TRIPP ELLIS

I showed him a picture of Anthony Williams on my phone. "This guy. He may have been shot in the parking lot."

Jacko's brow lifted with surprise. "Here?"

"It appears that way. You remember seeing him?"

Jacko studied the image. "That's the attorney they found burned to a crisp, right?"

"Yeah."

"I remember that guy. He was in here quite a bit. Big spender. The girls liked him."

I filled him in on the details of Anthony's credit card charges. "You remember anything about that night?"

Jacko thought for a moment. "Days run together here. Every day is the same. Tits, tits, and more tits. But hey, who's complaining?"

"Was Anthony with anybody?"

Jacko frowned. "I can't be sure, but I think he was here by himself."

"You know who danced for him that night?"

Jacko thought for another moment. His eyes surveyed the club. He pointed out a platinum blonde with hair that hung in a severe bob above her shoulders. She had the toned body of a real dancer. Definition in her thighs and abs. Perfect, petite perky peaks.

"Starr was one of his regulars." Jacko grabbed a passing waitress. "Be a doll and tell Starr to come see me when she finishes with her client."

The waitress grabbed a tray of drinks from the bar, then hustled to Starr, passed the message, then continued on, delivering cocktails.

"Can I get you anything while you wait?" Jacko asked.

It was a little early to start drinking, and we had a full day ahead. I could see Jack contemplating his options, but better judgment prevailed.

30

S tarr was interesting to talk to and even better to look at. She had full lips, green eyes, and smooth skin. "Yeah, I remember Tony coming in last week."

"What did you two talk about?" I asked.

"The usual stuff. Most guys come in here and complain about work, bitch about their wives, and try to make themselves sound important."

"Did he ever mention anything to you about Vinnie Farina?"

Starr shrugged. "I don't know. Honestly, I just smile, nod, and look pretty.

I told her Tony was dead, and she frowned. "That sucks. He was a good customer."

"Is that it?"

"What do you want from me? This is a job. I don't get emotionally attached to clients."

"Did he ever express concern for his safety?"

"No. He was the kind of guy that never worried about anything. He just knew it was all going to work out. I guess it didn't."

She didn't have much else to add. "If that's all, I need to get back to work."

We thanked her for her time, and she sauntered away.

"Starr is all business," Jacko said.

"I see that."

Before I could say my usual bit, Jacko cut me off. "I know the drill. I'll ask around, see if the girls saw anything in the parking lot. If something turns up, I'll let you know."

"Are you ever going to get security cameras around here?"

"Hell no! This isn't the kind of place that you want anybody having video evidence that you visited. If there are no cameras, there's no footage to subpoena. And you know how it is these days. If it's not on camera, it didn't happen."

I thanked Jacko for his hospitality, and we left the club. The blinding sun bounced off the sidewalk, and we squinted as our eyes adjusted.

My phone buzzed with a call from Denise. "I've got more information for you. Vinnie Farina was out of town the night Anthony Williams visited Forbidden Fruit. If that was the night he was murdered, then Vinnie has a solid alibi."

"Vinnie always seems to have a solid alibi," I grumbled. "Look into his two goons Dino and Enzo. See if you can figure out where they were."

"I'm on it."

I ended the call and dialed Isabella. The last charge on Anthony's credit card was at 12:47 AM Monday morning. He settled his tab, then headed to the parking lot. I asked Isabella to pinpoint any cell phones that may have been in the area at the time, specifically ones linked to Dino and Enzo.

"I'll see what I can find out," she said.

She sounded like she was in a rush and ended the call quickly.

The forensics guys had finished by the time we returned to the parking lot. We hopped into JD's Porsche and returned to the station to fill out after-action reports.

Isabella called me back as I was finishing up. "Cell phone records put Anthony Williams inside Forbidden Fruit until 12:59 AM. He's in the parking lot at 1:05 AM and stays there a few minutes. Then his cell phone goes off the grid. There are no other cellular devices in the parking lot at that time."

"So our shooter pops him, stuffs him in the trunk, and turns off Anthony's cell phone."

"Looks that way."

"Where were Enzo and Dino at that time?"

"I don't know. They don't keep cell phones in their names. I'm sure they're using prepaid cellulars and ditching them every few weeks."

"Thanks for the info."

"You got it."

"Things good on your end?"

"For the most part. It's a little hectic right now."

"Thanks for working me in."

"Not a problem." She ended the call.

"I'm beginning to think we've been looking at this the wrong way," JD said. "Maybe Anthony was the mistake, and Austin was the target."

"I think we need to have another conversation with the doctor's wife."

Denise poked her head into the conference room, and her emerald eyes met mine. "There's a phone call for you."

"Who is it?" I asked.

"Some girl."

I took the call at Denise's desk. "This is Deputy Wild."

"I hope it's okay that I'm calling you here. Addy threw away your card, so I didn't have your direct number."

"JoJo?"

She didn't say anything.

"How can I help you?"

"I've been thinking. Do you really think that Axel had something to do with that girl's disappearance?"

"I do."

"What would you need me to do?"

"I'd like to get him off the streets before he can hurt anybody else. You're not going to get in trouble, but tell me the truth. Did he provide you with drugs last night?"

"You swear you're not going to bust me?"

"I swear."

"Okay, yeah. He had some blow."

"Some?"

"Okay, a lot."

"What else did he have?"

"He said he had anything we wanted."

"Would you be willing to wear a wire and purchase drugs from him?"

She hesitated a moment. "I guess I can do that."

"While you're with him, see if you can find out any information about Zoe Brooks without being too obvious about it."

She was silent for a moment. "This is dangerous, isn't it?"

"It could be."

"What if he figures out I'm wearing a wire?"

"You'll be wearing a hidden camera concealed in a necklace. It would be extremely difficult for him to detect."

"Can I think about it?" she asked in a timid voice.

"Absolutely. But the longer we wait, the more difficult it's going to be to find Zoe Brooks."

"You think she's still alive?"

"I don't know. We have no reason to believe otherwise at the moment."

"What happens if something goes wrong?"

"We'll be nearby with a support team. The minute things even look like they're going bad, the team will rush in."

She paused for another moment. "Okay. Count me in."

I grinned. "Fantastic. You're doing the right thing."

"When do you want to do this?"

"Whenever you are available," I said.

"I guess I could do it tonight. What should I say?"

"Just text or call him and ask him if you can buy some party favors for you and your girlfriends tonight."

"You think he'll go for it?"

"That depends. Do you think he wants to see you again?"

"We fucked his brains out last night. Of course he wants to see us again."

"Tell him you want a little one-on-one time."

"I don't have to do anything with him, do I?"

"No. Of course not."

"Because after what you said about him, he kinda grosses me out."

"You just have to purchase drugs, and money has to change hands."

"What if he wants to exchange it for... you know?"

"Tell him you need a lot because you are going out tonight with a large group of girls who want to party."

"Okay."

"Can you come up to the station now, and we can put a plan in motion?"

31

JoJo joined us at the station and texted Axel that she needed a little nose candy. He responded: *[Swing by the apartment around 7 PM. Or I'll be at the bar from 8 PM onward.]*

JoJo looked at me for guidance. We sat in the conference room.

"Tell him you'll meet him at the apartment."

She responded.

Axel texted: *[How much do you need?]*

JoJo again looked at me for guidance. I told her, and she replied. [Quarter ounce, if you got it.]

[Wow. You girls can handle that much?]

[I have a lot of girlfriends.]

[You have funds for that? That's a little more than we can take out in trade.]

[No trade tonight. Aunt Flo came to visit.]

Axel texted a dollar amount.

JoJo showed me the screen.

"Tell him that's fine," I said.

She replied again.

I rounded up Erickson and Faulkner. We prepped the gear, donned bulletproof vests, and climbed into the surveillance van. As the time drew near, we followed JoJo to Axel's apartment.

I had given JoJo the same emerald necklace that we used in our previous sting operation with Denise. This time, I pumped the footage in through the large monitors in the surveillance van. We watched as JoJo climbed the steps to Axel's apartment and knocked on the door.

He greeted her with a smile and let her into the apartment.

The camera view was shaky. It didn't have image stabilization, and it moved every time the necklace swung from her collarbones.

The audio came through crystal clear.

Once JoJo was inside, Erickson and Faulkner hopped out of the van, rushed through the complex, and made their way up the steps to Axel's apartment. They took a position on either side of the door with a battering ram, ready to move in at a moment's notice.

"Are you sure you girls can handle this?" Axel asked. "The last thing I need is a bunch of sorority girls ODing on something I sold them."

"We're not going to OD. We can handle our high. Is it clean shit?"

"It's the same stuff you had last night."

"That was pretty clean."

"I only get the best stuff."

"Where do you get it?"

He scoffed. "I'm not telling you. Trade secret. But it's as pure as you can get. Never been stepped on."

They took a seat on the couch and Axel measured it out, weighing it on the scale so JoJo could see. "We good?"

"Looks good to me."

"Want a bump?"

"Don't mind if I do."

Axel handed JoJo a straw, and she tooted a fat rail. She sniffled, then blotted the residue on the glass coffee table with her finger and rubbed it on her gums.

"Told you it was good stuff. Let's see the cash."

JoJo dug into her purse and handed him a wad of crisp bills that we had given her.

Axel took the money and counted it, peeling off bill after bill.

We piled out of the van and rushed to meet the other deputies. I continued to watch the footage on my phone.

"You know, I can give you a little extra if you blow me," Axel said.

"What's the matter? Didn't you get enough last night?"

He smirked. "Maybe I want a second helping."

"Who did you have more fun with, me or Addy?"

He gave a political answer. "Who do you think?"

"You mind if I use the restroom first?"

"Sure, go ahead. Just down the hall."

JoJo climbed off the couch and headed down the hallway toward the master bedroom. There was a guest half-bath on the left. She pushed inside and ran the faucet. Then she whispered into the mic. "I'm not sucking this guy off."

I gave the signal to Erickson and Faulkner. They heaved the battering ram against the door, and the jam splintered. The door swung wide.

We stormed in, weapons in the firing position.

"Freeze!" I shouted. "Coconut County. You're under arrest!"

Axel nearly pissed himself.

There was the better part of a kilo on the coffee table. Axel reached his hand for a chrome pistol that rested beside the bag of nose candy.

"Don't even think about it!"

32

The apartment was loaded with goodies—a 65" flatscreen TV, surround sound, expensive furniture, a high-end mountain bike, a console gaming system, a desk with a dual-monitor setup. A couple of guitars occupied the corners—an acoustic and a Les Paul. Fine art canvases of naked women adorned the walls. It seemed that Axel had plenty of disposable income he couldn't claim on his tax return.

The kid was smarter than he looked. He stopped in his tracks and didn't pick up the weapon from the glass coffee table.

"Keep your hands in the air!" I shouted. "Stand up slowly and move away from the couch."

Several jumpy deputies with high-powered weapons can be pretty persuasive.

Axel stared down the angry barrels and complied.

Faulkner ratcheted the cuffs around his wrists.

"You can't just barge in here without a warrant."

JoJo emerged from the bathroom, made her way down the hall, and held up at the entrance to the living room. Her wide eyes surveyed the scene.

Axel scowled at her. "Fucking bitch! You set me up."

"Fuck you, creep. I didn't do anything."

Faulkner read Axel his rights and escorted him out of the apartment.

We searched the premises. The cocaine on the coffee table was enough to put him away for a considerable amount of time, compounded by the weapons charge. Drugs and guns always bump up the charges.

In the master bedroom, we found several items of women's clothing in the closet that likely belonged to Zoe Brooks. We also found a cell phone in a pink case. The battery was dead. I used a nearby charger to power it up. It took a few minutes to charge it enough to turn on.

It was Zoe's phone on her mother's plan.

In the closet, we also found a stash of pills that I figured for some type of amphetamine and another kilo of a powdery substance that I believed to be heroin. A field test kit indicated a preliminary positive for narcotics. The lab would test again to confirm the results.

We confiscated the goods, along with Zoe's belongings, and headed back to the station. I drove JoJo's car. The line of coke had launched her to the moon. Combined with the adrenaline, she was more than a little jittery. She was our responsibility, and I wasn't about to let her get behind the wheel.

Axel was processed, printed, and put into an interrogation room. We had the bust archived on video, and JoJo made a sworn affidavit. Her wide eyes darted about, and she rambled on, a mile a minute. "What happens now? I mean, when he gets out, he's gonna come after me."

"He's not getting out," I said.

"What if he makes bail?"

"My guess is bail will be set pretty high. But don't worry. If he gets out, we'll make arrangements to keep you safe."

"What kind of arrangements? I don't want to go into a protection program. I'll never see my family and friends again. I like my life just the way it is."

"Your life will stay just like it is. You did the right thing. This is gonna help us find Zoe."

"I hope so. I just got to thinking about that girl. I saw her picture on the news, and it just made me sick."

"We're going to put Axel away for a long time. Don't worry."

She nodded.

As a matter of protocol, and for liability purposes, she had to be evaluated by EMTs. She had a little tachycardia, which was par for the course with stimulants.

"The EMTs are going to take you to the ER to get checked out."

Her face crinkled. "I'm fine."

"You're wired."

"I'm already coming down."

"It's just a precaution."

"I'm not going to the ER. I'm fine."

I frowned at her.

"You can't make me go."

"You should think about quitting."

"I don't have a problem. I just do it for fun here and there."

"That's how it starts. Trust me. I know a lot of people who've gone down that path. It never ends well."

"I can totally handle my high."

"That's what everybody says."

She gave me the *I'm an invincible teenager* look.

"Just go with the EMTs and get checked out. You can pick up your car in the morning."

"Fine," she sighed. "Whatever."

She left with the EMTs.

JD and I had a little chat with Axel in the interrogation room.

33

Axel sat at the desk in the interrogation room with a tight jaw, his wrists cuffed in front of him. He glared at us as we entered. We took a seat across the table.

"You had no right to enter my apartment."

"To the contrary, we had reason to believe a crime was in progress," I said. "Last time I checked, dealing narcotics in the state of Florida was a crime. And I hate to inform you, but with the amount of illicit substances in your possession, you're looking at 30 years or more for drug trafficking."

Axel swallowed hard.

"Here's the deal. You give us information that leads us to Zoe Brooks, and maybe we can get the drug charges reduced."

Anger seethed in his eyes. The veins in his face bulged, and his cheeks reddened. "You people suck."

"Maybe you shouldn't do illegal things. There's a thought."

We stared at each other for a long moment.

"Where is Zoe Brooks?"

"I told you. I don't know. She moved out."

"There were plenty of her possessions in your apartment."

"She packed light."

"Cut the crap, Axel. Where is she?"

"How should I know?"

"Is she alive or dead?"

His face crinkled. "Why would you think she's dead?"

"Oh, I don't know," I said condescendingly. "The fact that nobody has seen her in a few weeks. Except for you. You're the last person to reportedly see her alive."

"I told you. She talked about traveling. She wanted to be a model in New York or some shit like that."

"You know what I think?"

"I don't care what you think."

"I think you gave her drugs. I think she OD'd. Maybe she died in your apartment, and you freaked out."

His face crinkled. "What are you talking about, man? You searched my apartment. She's not there."

"I don't know. Maybe you cut her into pieces, stuffed her into a bag, and dumped the remains."

A look of revulsion twisted on his face. "You're sick, dude. Anybody ever told you that?"

"30 years," I said, letting it hang there.

A thin mist of sweat formed on his skin.

"Since you won't talk about Zoe. Tell me where you're getting the drugs?"

"What drugs?"

I chuckled. "Just FYI, we have you on video selling cocaine to Josephine. The 2 kilos found in your apartment tested positive for narcotics with a field kit, as well as the pills." I paused. "You've never spent any time in prison, have you?"

He said nothing.

"It's no picnic. And the nature of your crime will put you in with some pretty tough offenders. Murderers, rapists, high-level dealers, gang bangers."

"I can hold my own."

"No you can't. You're gonna get eaten alive in there, kid. You know it, and I know it."

He tried to hide his obvious concern.

"I'll let you in on a little secret. The people you get your drugs from are going to be a little concerned. You're moving a lot of product. They know you're gonna be looking at serious time. And they'll think you'll be inclined to flip."

His face quivered.

"How long do you really think you're going to last in there?"

"As long as I keep my mouth shut, I'll last a long time. I want to speak with an attorney."

That was the end of the interview.

I shrugged and let out a dramatic sigh for effect. The chair squealed as I pushed away from the table. I stood up, strolled to the door, and knocked. A guard buzzed it open. Before we stepped outside, I said, "If you want to lessen your sentence, you'll talk to me about Zoe Brooks."

JD and I stepped into the hallway and were met shortly by Sheriff Daniels. He'd watched the whole thing from the observation room. "That little punk knows a lot more than he's saying."

"Maybe a couple days in the big house will give him a new perspective," I said.

Axel would be arraigned in the morning. With any luck, bail would be set high. But I wasn't holding my breath.

34

D aniels called the next morning. His gruff voice barked into the phone. It wasn't good news. "That little bastard got sprung. Judge Echols set bail at $50K."

"So Axel is out?"

"Yes. Guess which law firm represents him?"

"No way. Seriously?"

"Yep," Daniels said. "Evelyn Foster was at his arraignment this morning."

"The kid must have some serious cash stockpiled."

"Or he's got a big fish looking out for him."

"Interesting."

"Where are you with Austin and Anthony?"

"Square one," I said in a frustrated tone.

"And you've got no other leads on Zoe Brooks?"

"Not at the moment."

Daniels grumbled.

"Hey, these things don't solve themselves."

"Let me know when you've got something."

I ended the call and pulled myself out of bed. After breakfast, I called JD, and we decided to speak with Megan Williams again.

JD swung by the marina, and I hopped into the Porsche. "Any late-night trysts with Sloan?"

His face crinkled. "Hell no. I'm not playing second fiddle."

"Have you talked to her?"

"Not since we saw her at the club. She called and texted a few times, trying to explain. I didn't respond."

I gave him a look.

"I swear. I'm not getting involved in that nonsense."

"Were they really ever broken up?"

He shrugged. "She says she met him at the club because he wanted to talk."

"Are they back together now?"

"Who knows?"

Jack left it at that, and I didn't broach the subject again.

We caught up with Megan at her mansion in *Stingray Bay*.

"We have a few additional questions for you," I said when she greeted us at the front door.

"Certainly. Come on in."

She stepped aside and ushered us through the foyer into the living room and offered us a seat.

She looked a lot better than she did the other day. She'd had time to process and was trying to pick up the pieces. Though I had a sneaking suspicion, tears weren't far under the surface. Most people are barely keeping their head above water in the days and months after the death of a loved one.

"I'm beginning to believe your husband may have been the target all along," I said.

"So, that anonymous caller to the TV station was a hoax?"

"It appears that way. Anthony Williams was killed before your husband. I'll ask again, can you think of anyone who may have wanted to hurt Austin?"

She shook her head. "Like I told you, Austin didn't have any real enemies."

"And you never saw any indication that might lead you to believe he was having an affair?"

She shook her head. "We had a great marriage."

Her eyes brimmed.

"Do you know if he was into anything illegal?"

"Austin came to a full stop at stop signs. He drove the speed limit. He signaled to change lanes. Austin didn't break the law. He was by the book."

I was starting to feel like the cases were slipping away.

"Have you talked to his PA and his receptionist?" Megan asked.

"We have. Is there something specific you had in mind?"

"It's probably nothing. I didn't think of it the other day. But I remember Austin had an employee that gave him a little trouble."

"What do you mean by trouble?"

"She got fixated on him. At least, that's what he told me. He had to let her go. She stalked him for a while. She was calling here at the house. I had to get rude with her. When I did, she threatened me."

"What did she say?"

"I don't really recall the specifics of it. But she implied that she wanted me out of the picture and was willing to take me out herself."

"And you didn't think this was important?" I asked.

"It slipped my mind. It was a while ago."

"Are you sure your husband didn't have an affair with this woman?"

"Oh, no. Absolutely not!"

"How can you be so sure about that?"

"Because I trusted Austin. He told me there was never anything between them."

"What's this woman's name?"

"Stephanie Clark. She was his receptionist before Susan."

"You have her contact information?"

"I think I still have her number in my phone. I blocked that bitch. Her calls were incessant. I told her I'd call the police if she contacted us or came near my husband again. That was the last time I heard from her."

Megan texted Stephanie's contact information to me.

"We'll look into her. See what we can find," I said.

We thanked Megan and left. As we strolled the walkway to the Porsche, I called Denise. "Can you get background information on Stephanie Clark?"

35

"You're not going to believe where she works," Denise said.

She gave me the details listed on Stephanie's professional social media profile. She'd picked up another job as a receptionist in a dental office in the same building as Austin's plastic surgery clinic.

That set off alarm bells.

We returned to the professional building and looked for Dr. Peterson's Family Dentistry. It was located on the first floor across the atrium from Austin's plastic surgery clinic.

We pushed into the waiting room, and Stephanie Clark greeted us with a warm smile. "New patients?"

There were a few people waiting, flipping through magazines. An aquarium in the corner bubbled as colorful fish glided through the water. The sound of a dental drill hummed in the background.

Stephanie was easy on the eyes. Dark brown hair, royal blue eyes, sculpted features, and perfect teeth. She had a wonderful smile, but it wasn't reflected in her eyes. They were hollow. Some might say crazed. There was a sad desperation in them.

I flashed my badge. "I'd like to ask you a few questions about Dr. Williams."

Her smile faded, and a look of dread washed over her face. She swallowed hard. "It's just terrible what happened. I saw it on the news."

Our conversation drew the eyes of curious patients in the waiting room.

"Were you working that day?"

Stephanie grew uncomfortable in the hot seat. "I was. But I left at 5:30 PM."

"It's my understanding that you harassed Dr. Williams and made threats."

That flustered her. "What!?"

She glanced to the patients, and they averted their eyes.

"That's a mischaracterization."

"How would you characterize it?"

"As you can see, I'm working. This is not the ideal time."

"We can do this here, or we can do this down at the station," I said.

I had nothing on her that would justify bringing her in. But sometimes, a little intimidation never hurts.

She cleared her throat and swallowed again.

The phone rang, giving her a momentary break.

"If you'll excuse me, I need to take this."

She answered the call and booked an appointment, then returned her attention to us.

A hygienist passed by, opened the door, and called for Mrs. Diaz.

Mrs. Diaz lifted from her seat and greeted the dental assistant.

"How are you doing this afternoon?" the hygienist asked.

"I'm good."

"Right this way," the hygienist said, holding the door for Mrs. Diaz as she looked at us with curious eyes.

"Amy, I'm going to take a five-minute break," Stephanie said to the hygienist as she passed by with Mrs. Diaz. Stephanie's gaze returned to us. "Let's discuss this in the courtyard."

Stephanie pushed away from her desk and joined us in the waiting room. We followed her into the atrium and continued the conversation by a Koi pond.

"I never made threats against Dr. Williams or his wife. I may have gotten a little carried away and called him a few too many times at home."

"Were you involved in a sexual relationship?"

She hesitated for a moment. "You have to understand, I was in love with Dr. Williams. And Dr. Williams was in love with me."

"Is that so?"

"He was going to leave his wife."

"So, the relationship was serious."

"We discussed marriage."

I studied Stephanie carefully. I felt that she *believed* there was a relationship between the two and that Austin was in love with her. But I wasn't sure if that was really the case, or if she had an exaggerated memory of their interaction.

She seemed a little *intense*. The kind of girl that assumes marriage after one date.

"If you two had such a wonderful, budding relationship, what happened?"

"That bitch stole him away from me."

"Who?"

36

"Kayla!" Stephanie exclaimed.

"Austin's best friend's wife?"

"Yes!"

"You're sure about this?" I asked.

"I'm positive."

"You have any kind of proof?"

"I saw them with my own eyes. That might not be proof enough for you, but it's proof enough for me."

"You saw them out together?"

She hesitated a moment and shifted uncomfortably. "Well, I followed them to that crappy little motel, the Seahorse Sands."

"Seahorse Shores?"

"Yeah, whatever."

"And you're sure they were going there to hook up?"

"Why else would anyone stay in that fleabag? He wasn't giving her a cleaning and checking. Well, he may have been filling a few cavities."

"I'm kinda surprised you didn't tell his wife," I said.

"I thought about it. Then I figured, fuck her. Let her figure it out on her own. I guess she never did."

"Did it make you mad when you found out Austin was giving it to Kayla?" JD asked.

"I was devastated. You're damn right I was mad."

"Mad enough to kill him?" I asked.

She looked at us like we were idiots. "Why would I wait a year to take revenge on that bastard?"

I shrugged. "Maybe you were being patient."

"I think what happened to Austin is terrible. And it makes me sad. But I've moved on and forgiven him. I've got a new man in my life, and if you haven't noticed, I am currently engaged," she said, wiggling her finger displaying a sparkling diamond.

"Who's the lucky man?"

She smiled. "Dr. Peterson."

That seemed to be her MO.

"Congratulations to you two love birds," I said.

"Thank you."

"We may have more questions for you. Don't leave town."

"Hello. I'm getting married next week. I'll most certainly be leaving town. We're going to the Bahamas for our honeymoon."

She was giddy with anticipation.

My interest in her as a suspect was fading. Kayla's husband had jumped to the top of my list.

We left the professional building, and I called Kayla's cell phone. I wanted to speak with her before going after Brandon.

She answered after a few rings. "This is Kayla."

"This is Deputy Wild with Coconut County. We met the other night."

"Of course. What can I do for you?"

"We'd like to ask you a few follow-up questions. You have a moment to meet?"

"I'm at Highland Village right now. I could meet you back at my home in an hour."

"We'd like to speak privately. How about we meet you at the food court? The pizza by the slice joint. Say 20 minutes?"

"Okay. Sure. I'll see you then."

In the parking lot, there were still clumps of melted rubber from Austin's tires stuck to the asphalt. We hopped into JD's Porsche and hustled to the open-air mall. It was full of luxury boutiques. Expensive cars lined the parking lot, and couture bags dangled from manicured fingers. There were plenty of long legs, stiletto heels, and short skirts. Coconut Key's elite engaging in retail therapy.

We grabbed a couple slices of cheese pizza and waited for Kayla. It wasn't bad for mall pizza. Cheesy, doughy goodness. But it didn't hold a candle to Big Tony's.

The food court was half full, and sun filtered through the potted trees. It was a good place to sit and watch pretty people.

Kayla arrived with several bags in tow, wearing dark Chanel sunglasses. She wore a tight black low-cut dress and a wide-brimmed hat. She could have been a movie star. Pouty lips, slick with gloss, a figure to kill for, a gaze that smoldered.

We stood to greet her, then took a seat.

"So, what's going on?" Kayla asked. "Do you have any new leads?"

"There have been some interesting developments," I said in an understated tone. "What can you tell me about your relationship with Austin?"

"What do you mean?"

"You know what I mean."

She swallowed hard and squirmed. "He's been a dear friend of my husband's since grade school."

"We know you were having an affair."

"What!?" She feigned offense.

"Are you trying to protect your husband by denying it?"

"No. I'm not trying to protect anybody."

"Stop giving me the runaround and come clean."

She took a deep breath. After a long pause, she said, "Okay. Yes. We were having an affair."

"Why didn't you say something sooner?"

"What was I going to say? *Oh, by the way, Megan, I've been fucking your husband for the last year and a half?*"

"You could have called me directly."

"It would still have come out."

"The truth always does, sooner or later."

She frowned.

"And you never once considered that your husband may be responsible for Austin's death."

She hesitated again, conflicted. "Yes, that crossed my mind. But he was at home with the kids."

"While you were at *yoga class,*" I said in air quotes.

"Okay, I wasn't at yoga class."

"Care to tell me where you were?"

"I was with Austin at the office."

I lifted a curious brow. "The night of the murder?"

"Yes."

"What time did you leave?"

"I left my house at 6:30 PM. I got to his office around 7 PM. We did our thing. I left at 7:45 and caught the tail end of my yoga class, then came home."

"So you were the last person to see him alive?"

She hesitated. "I guess so."

"Did you see anyone suspicious in the parking lot?"

"No. I mean, I looked around to see if Brandon had followed me up there. I was always a little paranoid about that. I rushed to my car and left."

"But Austin stayed behind."

"Yes. We never liked to leave at the same time. I see an acupuncturist in the same building. Gives me plausible deniability."

"You know I'm sure all the sneaking around added to the thrill, but don't you think being honest would have been a better policy?"

She shrank with guilt. "Do you really think my husband killed Austin?"

"I'm beginning to think so. Yes."

She sighed, and her head fell into her hands. A tear rolled down her cheek from behind the dark sunglasses. She sniffled and tried to hold back the sobs. The dam finally burst. "This is all my fault. I got him killed."

I wasn't going to sugarcoat anything. "Maybe."

She tried to pull it together.

I handed her a napkin. She lifted her glasses and blotted the tears away. Then she glanced around to see who was in the food court and if anyone was watching.

"Does your husband own any guns?"

She shook her head. "No."

"Are you sure?"

"It's possible he bought one without my knowledge."

"I need you to do me a favor. I need access to bank statements, credit cards, phone records."

"Why?"

"I'm looking for anything that might tie him to the crime.
Have you noticed any unusual withdrawals?"

She thought for a moment. "He did move $50,000 out of one
of our accounts, but he said that was to invest in crypto. I
don't really pay attention to the finances."

"Where's Brandon right now?"

37

B randon looked surprised to see us. He pulled open the door to his Stingray Bay mansion and forced a smile. "Deputies... What can I do for you?"

I had asked Kayla not to give him any advance notice, and it appeared that she kept her mouth quiet. She agreed to assist with our investigation. It was clear that her romance with Austin was more than a casual tryst. The two had been intimately involved for quite a while, and according to her, they were both contemplating leaving their marriages.

"We have a few follow-up questions," I said.

"Sure. Anything I can do to help. I'm just devastated over this. Austin was such a dear friend. It still hasn't fully hit me yet.

"Mind if we come inside?" I asked.

"Oh, sure. My bad." He stepped aside and ushered us in.

Travertine tile lined the floor, and the walls were painted light beige. There were dark hardwoods in the living room, and the mansion had a cozy, earth-tone feel.

"Can I get you guys anything to drink? Water, beer, whiskey?"

We declined, but Brandon poured himself a glass of whiskey and took a sip.

He offered us a seat on the couch, and we obliged.

I didn't have anything concrete. I couldn't place him at the scene of the crime. Kayla had shown me their bank account on her phone, and there was a cash withdrawal for $50,000. That was it. That $50,000 could have gone anywhere, to anyone.

I had a gut feeling, and it had intensified the moment we stepped inside Brandon's house. He tried to play it cool, but his nervous fidgeting only increased my suspicion. If we were going to get this guy, we needed to force an error.

"Do you know where your wife was at the time of Austin's death?"

"Yeah. She was at yoga class. I thought we had already established that."

"We did. I'm just asking you."

"That's where she told me she was. I have no reason to think otherwise."

"You guys have a good relationship?"

"We have a great relationship."

"Really?"

"Absolutely. 100%. I love her like no other."

"I don't doubt that. She's a beautiful woman."

He grinned with pride. "Isn't she?"

"I'd do anything to keep a woman like that."

"Damn straight."

"It would just kill me if I thought my woman was fooling around."

Brandon shook his head. "I don't even want to think about something like that. I don't think I could take it."

"Losing a woman like that could make a man go insane," I said. "Especially if you lost her to a best friend."

His face tightened.

I stared him down, and he took a nervous sip of his whiskey.

"When did you find out Kayla was having an affair with Austin?" I asked.

Brandon almost choked on his whiskey. His face crinkled. "What!?"

"We're past that, aren't we?" I said flatly.

"I don't know what you're talking about."

"Kayla's been having an affair with Austin for over a year now. We know you know."

He shifted nervously.

"What did you do with the $50,000 in cash you withdrew from the bank?"

Brandon swallowed hard. "I want an attorney."

"You're not under arrest." We didn't have to stop questioning him. "Who did you pay to kill Austin?"

"I didn't pay anybody to kill my friend."

"What did you do with the $50,000?"

"How do you have that information?"

Kayla stormed in through the front door. Her high heels clacked against the tile as she marched into the living room, tears streaming down her cheeks. "You killed him!"

"I didn't kill anybody." Brandon stood up and looked at us. "I want you to leave. Now! Get out of my house."

Kayla shrieked, "You're a murderer! I fucking hate you."

She beat on his chest with her fists.

"And you're a whore!"

Anger got the best of him. He shoved her away.

Kayla toppled to the ground and slid across the hardwoods.

I drew my handcuffs. "You're under arrest for domestic violence."

"She assaulted me," Brandon protested. "You saw her. I was defending myself."

38

It was just the excuse we needed to take Brandon into custody.

JD slapped the cuffs around Brandon's wrists, and I called for a patrol unit to take him to the station.

Kayla wasn't done, and she took the opportunity to go off on her husband. "I should have left you a long time ago. You're not half the man that Austin was."

Brandon's face reddened.

"He could make me feel ways that you never could."

She proceeded to rattle off all the various locations where they had hooked up and all the dirty little things they had done. She stuck the knife in and twisted it.

Rage boiled under Brandon's skin, and his eyes blazed into her.

"You're going to spend the rest of your miserable life behind bars! And I'll be out here fucking everything."

Brandon was about to explode.

"Just admit it. You killed him. You killed him because you know you just didn't measure up." She measured out about 2 inches between her thumb and index finger and wiggled her hand in front of his face.

I didn't think it was possible for Brandon's cheeks to get any redder, but they did. His eyes brimmed, and I almost felt sorry for the guy.

Then Kayla went for the gut punch.

She pulled out her phone, launched the photos app, and scrolled through the library. She pulled up a video and played it for Brandon.

Moans and groans and slurping sounds emanated from the device. I had a pretty good idea what was going on. I caught a glimpse of Kayla's head bobbing up and down while she captured selfie footage of the intimate act. Her wet lips worked their magic. "I've got plenty more where that came from. You want to see them all?"

Brandon's eyes brimmed, and the muscles in his jaw flexed. "It's a good thing you got that video because you're never gonna sleep with him again."

Kayla's eyes filled. "Because you killed him."

I didn't put her up to it, but Kayla was trying to piss him off and get him to the point where he might let something slip. He looked like he was about to take credit for Austin's demise but kept his mouth shut.

Erickson and Faulkner arrived, and we escorted Brandon out of the house and stuffed him into the back of the patrol car.

"What happens now?" Kayla asked, wiping the tears from her eyes.

"All we have on him is a domestic violence charge. I need to get a confession out of him."

"You let me know what you need. I will help you in any way I can."

"We appreciate your cooperation."

We followed the patrol car to the station. Brandon was processed, printed, and put into an interrogation room. We let him sit for a long time as we filled out paperwork.

By the time we entered the interrogation room, Brandon looked gutted. He sat at the table slumped, his eyes teary, his expression empty like a man that had his soul ripped out.

Watching your wife blow your best friend will drain the life out of you.

We took a seat across from him without saying anything for a few moments.

"I didn't think she hated me that much," he finally said as he slumped in his chair. "You gotta really hate somebody to say those things."

"You had your best friend killed," I said flatly.

He erupted, "Because he was fucking my wife!"

It just slipped out.

I was stunned.

Brandon realized what he had said after he said it. But there was no taking it back now.

"I love her, man. I just don't know how this went so wrong. I mean, Austin was my best friend. How could he do that to me? Best friends don't do that to each other, do they?"

He just couldn't wrap his head around the whole thing. His eyes filled, and tears streamed down his cheek. The big guy sobbed for a few minutes.

"Who did you hire to kill Brandon?" I asked.

He was silent for a moment, then he looked up at us. "I don't know his name. I met him in a bar one night, and we got to talking. I had a few drinks and needed to vent. I told him my wife was having an affair with my best friend. He said he could fix that. Of course, I was intrigued. He said he could take care of one or both of them." Brandon frowned and shook his head. "At first, I was appalled by the idea. But then I got to thinking about it. And the more I thought about it, the better it sounded. I don't know what I was thinking."

"You weren't."

He frowned.

"What bar?"

"Dunsel."

"Can you describe the guy?"

"Yeah. He was mid to late 20s. Short brown hair. Mustache. Narrow face. Blue eyes."

"I'll have you work with our sketch artist."

He nodded. "If I help you, can we make a deal?"

"I'll see what we can do. You know how to get in touch with this guy?"

"He gave me a phone number."

"Do you have a name? What did you call him?"

"He told me to call him Mr. X."

"How did you pay Mr. X?"

"You know. The cash."

"You withdrew the cash from the bank and gave it to Mr. X. Where?"

"I put it in a backpack, and I met him at the bar. It was really simple."

"Okay. Here's what you're gonna do. You're gonna call Mr. X and arrange another hit."

Brandon's eyes rounded. "I am?"

"This time, you tell him you want your wife dead. Tell him your little plan backfired. Now she wants a divorce."

39

I texted Mr. X from Brandon's phone and waited for a reply.

And waited...

And waited...

"You sure this is the right number?" I showed the screen to Brandon.

"I'm positive. I'm sure he's using a burner phone. Maybe he ditched it already. I would have."

It would be foolish for a professional hitman to keep the same phone for more than one client. Too easy to connect to multiple homicides.

I sent a text message from my phone to Isabella and asked her to track Mr. X's phone. She replied a few minutes later that it was off the grid. It could have been turned off, or it could have been discarded.

"What happens now?" Brandon asked.

"I'm going to hang on to your phone and wait for your hitman to call back."

"What if he doesn't?"

"We'll get him. It's only a matter of time."

The statement may have been a little on the optimistic side, but I was a firm believer that you could manifest your own reality to a degree. The power of positive thinking.

Daniels poked his head into the interrogation room. "In the hall, now. We have a problem."

We left Brandon and joined Daniels.

"You two need to get over to the Coconut Club apartments. That little punk is dead."

My brow lifted with surprise. "What!?"

"I don't think this was a random coincidence. That dirtbag was our only connection to Zoe Brooks. Go see what you can find out."

We rushed out of the station and hopped into the Porsche. By the time we arrived at the Coconut Club apartments, the parking lot was flooded with emergency vehicles. Red and blue lights flickered, and deputies milled about. We hopped out and hustled up the steps to Axel's apartment. Camera flashes spilled out.

Mendoza and Robinson hovered by the doorway.

"What happened?" I asked.

"Neighbor passed by and saw that the door was ajar." He pointed to a blonde talking to Faulkner. "Then, she noticed the bloody paw prints." He pointed to crimson cat prints on the concrete leading away from Axel's door.

We stepped around the paw prints and pushed inside. Brenda hovered over the body. Axel lay on the floor in the living room, his cold, dead eyes staring blankly at the ceiling. His shirt blossomed red with two gunshot wounds. His skin was pale, and his lips almost translucent. All the blood had pooled around the corpse and stained the carpet. Crimson paw prints dotted the living room.

"You know what time this happened?" I asked.

"Maybe 2 to 4 hours ago," Brenda said. "He's pretty fresh. Looks like a small caliber. 9mm, possibly. No shell casings."

"Looks professional," JD said.

I glanced around the apartment. Nothing appeared to be missing. The guitars were still in the corners. The flatscreen display was still there. I was pretty sure this wasn't a robbery gone wrong.

I stepped out and talked to the blonde. She wore gray bike shorts, a pink sports bra, and white sneakers. She had short hair, brown eyes, and a narrow face.

"It sent a chill down my spine when I saw the bloody paw prints. I poked my head inside, and there he was. I called the Sheriff's Department right away."

"You remember hearing anything? Gunshots?"

She shook her head. "This must have happened before I came home. I was out for a run."

"And you didn't see anyone suspicious?"

She shook her head.

I took her contact information, and we canvassed the area, banging on neighboring doors. Nobody had seen or heard anything.

Or they weren't saying.

"I think somebody got a little concerned about Axel's recent arrest," JD muttered.

I stepped back inside the apartment and knelt beside the body, trying to avoid stepping in the bloodstains. I pulled on a pair of nitrile gloves and fished Axel's phone from his pocket. I used his face ID to unlock the device, then I scrolled through his recent calls and texts.

He had deleted everything.

A savvy drug dealer gets in the habit of deleting messages as they come in. He had an encrypted messaging app. It was empty as well. The messages had been set to disappear after half an hour.

I texted Isabella and had her pull the data for the phone. I was particularly interested in the recent calls and messages.

It didn't take long for Isabella to respond.

He'd received calls and texts from several different numbers. But the encrypted messaging app made it impossible to see who he had exchanged those messages with. There was no way to decipher the content.

Isabella texted: *[I'll look into these contacts and get back with you.]*

The forensic team dusted for prints. Brenda and her crew bagged the body. The deputies sealed the apartment and taped it off.

Axel's cat returned, and her paws were crusted with crimson. She was surprisingly friendly. I was in the habit of collecting rescue animals, but I did not need another pet.

The cat's name sparkled on her collar, encrusted with jewels. Perhaps faux diamonds, perhaps real. Brenda took Shasta back to the lab to evaluate the bloodstains and collect any other evidence from the cat. She assured me she'd find the proper forever home for Shasta.

We left and headed back to the station. After paperwork, we decided to blow off steam at *Waves*. It was a beach-themed bar with an outdoor pool and sand volleyball courts. It was a new bar, and was trying to compete with *Tide Pool*.

Pretty people frolicked in the pool, and fit beauties batted the volleyball over the net. Sand clung to wet skin. Pert bottoms jiggled. Fleshy mounds bounced. The outdoor patio wasn't a bad place to have a drink.

Still, we both preferred *Tide Pool*.

"That punk hires the best criminal defense firm on the island, gets sprung, and is dead a few hours later," JD said. "This has trouble written all over it."

He took a sip of his whiskey and focused on the volleyball court, trying to let it all fade away. But no matter how much we tried to relax, Zoe Brooks was always at the forefront of our minds.

The waitress had just delivered the second round when Brandon's phone buzzed my pocket.

40

I pulled out the device and looked at the text message from Mr. X. *[Who's the target?]*

I responded as Brandon: [My wife has become a pain in the ass.]

[I thought you loved her?]

[It's become clear that she doesn't love me. She wants a divorce.]

[Give her one. It's cheaper.]

[I'm not so sure about that.]

There was no communication for a few minutes.

[Are you sure you want this done?]

[Positive.]

[It can't be undone.]

[That's the whole point, isn't it?]

[You're lucky. I was about to ditch this phone.]

[Lucky is the man whose wife doesn't cheat on him.]

[Look at it like a gift. You now have the opportunity to explore other options.]

[Can you take care of the problem, or not?]

A few more minutes went by without a response.

[Meet me at the same location to discuss this further. Tomorrow. 8 PM.]

He was avoiding clear language for obvious reasons.

I continued to egg him on. [Should I bring payment?]

[You can if you like.]

I didn't want to push the issue and spook him.

He called the phone a moment later, clearly wanting to confirm that he was actually speaking with Brandon.

My plan was about to go awry.

I had to take the call. He'd get suspicious if I didn't.

I swiped the screen, held the phone to my ear, and did my best impersonation of Brandon. "If you don't want to do it, I can find somebody else."

"That won't be necessary," he said. "I just want to meet face-to-face and make sure this is what you want."

"It's what I want."

"If you say so." He paused. "We'll talk tomorrow. 8 PM. You know where."

He ended the call, and I instantly dialed Isabella from my phone. "I need you to trace the last call that Brandon's phone received."

With a few keystrokes, she pulled up the data and gave me the address where the call originated. "Prepaid cellular, currently at 721 Royal Tern Lane. The house belongs to Spencer Tanner." Her fingers tapped the keys again. "27 years old. Single. No priors."

"That's interesting."

"Served four years in the Army, and is currently working as a delivery driver for Overnight Parcel Express."

"Thank you."

"You're welcome. Now go bag that guy."

I grinned. "You got it."

I couldn't use the information Isabella gave me to get a warrant. We'd have to pull the records through legitimate means, and that would take time. But it did allow us to take a trip by Royal Tern and get eyes on the suspect's residence. We left *Waves* and did a drive-by.

JD pulled to the curb a few houses down, and we kept eyes on the house, hoping to catch a glimpse of the perp. We weren't very inconspicuous in a lava orange convertible, but at this time of night, nobody was paying much attention.

There were a few lights on in the house, and now and then, I saw a figure pass by the window. It was a tiny little house with a gravel shoulder in front. A narrow drive, overgrown with weeds, led to a carport. There was an old Nissan Pathfinder out front with a weathered hood—the paint bleached from the sun and the clear-coat long stripped away. Steps led to a small porch, and awnings hung over the windows. A bike was chained to the railing along the porch, and there was a propane barbecue grill out front.

We probably sat there for half an hour before Mr. X exited through the front door. He shuffled across the lawn, hopped into the Pathfinder, and drove away.

I got a decent look at him.

He was just as Brandon had described. Slender, short brown hair, narrow face, and a mustache.

"Want to follow him?" JD asked.

"No point," I said. "I don't want to take a chance of spooking him. We'll get him tomorrow."

We watched the maroon Pathfinder turn at the corner and disappear.

JD cranked up the engine, flipped on the lights, and pulled away from the gravel shoulder. We went in the opposite direction at the corner and cruised back to the marina at *Diver Down*. I told Jack I'd call him in the morning, hopped out, and hustled down the dock to the *Avventura*. Buddy greeted me with a wagging tail and a slobbering tongue. I took the Jack Russell out for a walk and enjoyed the cool night air.

The next day, we sprung Brandon from the holding pod. We gave him a polo shirt that had a camera and microphone hidden in one of the buttons. There was a wireless transmitter and a battery the size of a nickel sewn into the fabric. It sent the footage to an app on my phone.

We did a brief check of the equipment in the conference room. Everything seemed to be in working order.

"Here's the deal," I said. "I need confirmation from Mr. X that he's agreeing to kill your wife for the agreed-upon sum. Don't be too obvious about it, but don't make it too vague either."

"What if he doesn't want to talk about it?" Brandon asked.

"That's the whole point of the meeting. He wants to sniff you out. See if anything's funny. Don't flinch. Don't hesitate. Don't act nervous."

"Telling me not to act nervous is just making me nervous."

I sighed.

"I'm not an actor, okay."

"No, you're just a guy who paid another guy to kill his best friend," JD muttered.

Brandon scowled at him.

"You'll be fine," I assured. I stared him dead in the eye. "If you do anything to tip him off, or screw this up in any way, I will personally see to it that you get the maximum sentence possible. Are we clear?"

Brandon's nervous eyes looked at mine. He nodded. "Clear."

41

E rickson and Faulkner dressed in plain clothes and made their way toward *Dunsel*. JD and I took the surveillance van and drove by Brandon's house.

We picked up his car, and I gave him a backpack with the *buy* money. "We're going to be right behind you in the van. Try anything funny, or try to run, so help me..."

He raised his hands innocently. "I'm cooperating."

We let him drive to the bar, following behind him.

He turned into the parking lot at *Dunsel*, and we weren't far behind. I pulled up the feed from his hidden camera on the monitors inside the surveillance van as well as my phone. We sat in the parking lot and watched as Brandon stepped inside the hole-in-the-wall.

It was a dim little club a couple blocks off Oyster Avenue. There was a row of booths to the left, and the bar spanned the length of the establishment on the right except for a small area near the entrance with a jukebox and a quarter pool table. The restrooms were in the back.

True to its name, *Dunsel* was pretty useless—your standard neighborhood bar that was only good for one thing. Cheap drinks. You could unload your problems on the bartender, and he would pretend to listen. Tourists would stop in every now and then, but it was mainly hard-core locals. Guys that would show up at open and would sit at the bar until close. It was a place you went to drown your sorrows, or in Brandon's case, find someone who'd eliminate your sorrows for a price.

Brandon looked around the bar, then took a seat at the counter. He muttered into the mic, "He's not here."

He ordered a drink. The bartender poured a glass of whiskey, slid it across the counter, and Brandon downed it without hesitation. He nodded for another glass. It was the last chance at real whiskey he'd have.

Inmates made their own swill—*pruno, raisin jack, juice, brew, hooch*. They'd ferment fruit, adding sugar and yeast from bread or rolls. They'd hide it away and hope the guards didn't find it or smell it when they burped the bags to let the fermentation gasses out. It was nasty stuff that would turn your stomach. But it would give you a buzz. A sour, rancid buzz. If you drank it, you'd never have to prove your courage in any other way. I'd even heard stories of inmates setting up stills and distilling spirits. But none of it had the smooth texture of a fine whiskey.

8 o'clock rolled around. No sign of Mr. X.

8:15 PM came and went...

Then 8:30...

I was just about to lose hope when the maroon Pathfinder pulled into the parking lot. Spencer, a.k.a. Mr. X, hopped out and gave a cautious glance around before strolling inside.

He saw Brandon at the bar and took a seat next to him.

"What will it be?" the bartender asked.

"I'll have what he is having. And put it on his tab."

The bartender poured a glass of whiskey and slid it across the counter.

Mr. X took the glass, looked around the bar, then took a sip.

"You're late," Brandon said.

"Shit happens. You got the money?"

Brandon nodded. "In the backpack."

$50,000 lay against the footrest in a black backpack. Mr. X reached down, picked it up, and looked inside. He gave a cursory glance, then set it back down.

"Do we have a deal?" Brandon asked.

I waited on the edge of my seat for his reply. But I needed more clarity than that. He needed to agree to murder in no uncertain terms.

Mr. X surveyed Brandon carefully. Then he looked back to the booth where Erickson and Faulkner sat, drinking beer.

"I gotta take a leak." Mr. X took another swig of his whiskey, then pushed away from the bar and ambled toward the restrooms. When he passed by Erickson and Faulkner, he gave them both a long hard look.

They tried to ignore him, but Faulkner locked eyes with him for a moment before glancing away.

Mr. X continued on and pushed into the restroom.

"Something's wrong," Brandon said into the mic.

I wanted him to shut up, but he didn't have an earbud. I couldn't communicate with him.

Brandon fidgeted nervously.

Mr. X emerged from the restroom a few minutes later, then walked the length of the bar. He took another look at Erickson and Faulkner, then he kept walking straight past Brandon and stepped outside. He hustled to the Pathfinder, hopped in, and drove away.

"Son-of-a-bitch," JD muttered.

We hopped out of the surveillance van once Mr. X was gone and hustled into the bar.

"What the hell happened?" I asked. "You signal him?"

Brandon raised his hands innocently, his eyes wide. "No. I didn't do anything. He knew."

Erickson and Faulkner joined us.

"I think he made me," Faulkner said.

"What do you mean?" I asked.

"I wrote that guy a ticket last week. I think he recognized me."

My jaw tensed.

"Sorry, guys," Faulkner said. "Luck of the draw."

42

I texted Mr. X from Brandon's phone. [Why did you take off?]

[There were cops in the bar.]

[So what?]

[They were looking at me. You trying to set me up?]

[No. What are you talking about?]

He never texted back.

"What do you want to do now?" JD asked.

"You've got my statement," Brandon said. "Isn't that enough?"

"The case would be a hell of a lot stronger if we had something to tie him to the murders. You're not exactly the most credible witness in the world. You'll say anything to shift blame."

"I didn't kill anybody."

"Co-conspirator. That's a word you will become intimately familiar with."

Brandon's sworn statement was enough for us to get a warrant. Echols signed off on it, and within 45 minutes, we were at Spencer's door, decked out in tactical gear.

His Pathfinder wasn't in the driveway, so I figured he wasn't at home. But I gave a courtesy knock anyway and announced our presence. "Coconut County! We have a warrant."

Erickson and Faulkner heaved the battering ram against the door. It swung wide, splintering shards of wood. We stormed into the house with weapons drawn, clearing the corners and securing the area.

There was a small kitchen to the left, and the foyer opened into the living room. A flatscreen TV sat atop an entertainment center with a stereo and video game console. Black lacquer end tables framed the black leather couch, and a full ashtray sat atop a glass coffee table with a few empty beer bottles.

We advanced down the hallway and cleared the guest bedroom and bathroom, then pushed into the master bedroom. We turned the place upside down, pulling out drawers, flipping over mattresses, checking pillows, looking in closets, rummaging through jacket pockets, and checking air vents. We searched all the usual places but didn't find any weapons.

No knives, no guns, no 9mm ammunition.

No hard evidence to connect Spencer to the murders.

There were several items of mail on the kitchen table—utility bills, credit card bills, bank statements, and a bill for a self-storage unit. The unit number was visible through the window.

I didn't even need to open the mail. I called Daniels and asked him to get a warrant for the storage unit.

Mendoza and Robinson stayed behind at Spencer's house in case he returned. We headed to the storage unit, and Daniels met us there with a warrant in hand.

It was a plain three-story concrete building with a keypad for 24-hour access. The office was open 9 AM-5 PM, Monday through Friday. I dialed the number on the door, hoping to get in touch with the manager.

The phone rang and went to voicemail.

I left a message.

We waited for a call back that never came. I didn't really want to smash the glass entry door.

Fortunately, I saw a tenant in the hallway.

I flashed my badge and she let us in.

"What's the access code?" I asked.

"1429."

I knew we'd need it to access the different levels. We flooded into the hallway. The place was a maze of concrete passages lined with corrugated blue rollup doors, each with its own padlock. Fluorescent overheads bathed the halls in a sterile glow.

We took the elevator up to the second floor, and I had to punch in the code to gain access. We spilled out of the elevator, and I scanned the signs, then followed the path to Spencer's unit, #217. Faulkner snipped off the padlock with a pair of shears and lifted the rolling door to the 10x10 unit. It clattered, echoing down the hallways.

There were boxes of books and old magazines, an exercise bike, a couple pieces of ratty furniture—typical storage items. Most people pay more in storage fees than the stuff is worth.

Multiple outfits hung from a clothes rack against the wall. Black long sleeve shirts, navy blue jumpsuits, black jeans, multiple pairs of shoes. A full-length vanity mirror leaned against the corrugated wall. A 56" tall red rolling, 10-drawer tool chest crouched nearby.

This was a dressing area.

I started sifting through the drawers and found the mother load—9mm ammunition, several knives, a few black ski masks, nitrile gloves, rope, wire, and various tools. There were paper towels, wipes, and jugs of bleach nearby. In another drawer, I found various disguises—wigs, mustaches, and fake glasses.

"Something tells me this might not be this clown's first rodeo," JD said.

"We may have a bona fide hitman," I said.

This was all good circumstantial evidence. But we still didn't have the murder weapon. We confiscated the evidence, and Daniels had put a BOLO out on the suspect.

I stepped into the hallway, feeling somewhat accomplished.

The elevator dinged, and the doors slid open. Spencer stepped off and rounded the corner, heading toward the unit. His eyes widened with terror when he saw us. He spun around and darted back toward the elevator.

43

I sprinted after the scumbag and rounded the corner. Spencer got to the elevator just as the doors were closing. He stuck a hand between the doors, tripping the sensor. They slid back open, and he rushed onto the elevator.

I drew my weapon and took aim at his back. "Freeze! Put your hands in the air!"

I moved cautiously toward the elevator as the door started to close again.

Spencer hesitated a moment and put his hands in the air, still facing the far wall. Then he made a bad decision. He spun around, grabbed a pistol from his waistband, and took aim.

I squeezed my trigger.

My pistol hammered against my palm. Muzzle flash flickered from the barrel, and the tangy scent of gunpowder wafted toward my nostrils. The deafening bang echoed throughout the narrow concrete hallways, piercing my ears.

I put two bullets into Spencer's sternum.

Volcanoes of blood erupted from his chest as he fell back against the wall.

His eyes rounded.

His pistol dropped to the ground, and he coughed up blood as the elevator doors slid shut.

I tapped the call button before they closed.

Crimson blood streaked the far wall as Spencer slid to the ground.

I moved inside, hit the emergency stop, then kicked Spencer's weapon out of reach.

The buzzer rang incessantly.

Spencer gurgled for breath as his lungs filled with fluid. He coughed up blood, and his last breath rattled out. His body went still, and his fixed eyes stared straight ahead.

I knelt beside the scumbag and felt for a pulse.

By this time, the other deputies were right behind me.

I frowned and shook my head. He'd still be alive if he wasn't such an idiot. But maybe he felt going out, guns blazing, was a better alternative to life in prison. I figured he was coming back to the storage unit to clear out the evidence. Or maybe he was gonna stash the pistol here. Who knows?

Brenda and the forensics team arrived. Dietrich snapped photos, and the scene was documented. Blood pooled around the body, reflecting the overhead lights in the elevator. Camera flashes flooded out.

The 9mm was logged into evidence along with the other items. The lab could run ballistics, and hopefully, we'd get a match, putting this case to rest for good.

Paris texted. *[I heard there was a shooting at Coconut Storage.]*

[You heard correctly.]

[Care to share anything on the record?]

[Not particularly.]

[I heard the victim could be a hitman.]

[A victim of his own stupidity.]

[So, is the deceased a hitman?]

[I'll let you know when I have confirmation.]

By the time we wrapped up, Paris and a few other news crews were outside. They grabbed footage of the emergency vehicles and flashing lights. They all waited to capture a glimpse of Spencer's body rolled out on a gurney, zipped in a body bag. That was the *money shot.*

"Deputy Wild," Paris shouted. "Can you confirm the identity of the victim?"

There was that word again. Spencer was anything but a victim. He was a cold blooded killer.

"Not at this time," I said.

We hopped into the Porsche and drove away.

Back at the station, we filled out after-action reports, and I surrendered my duty weapon as usual. It was time for a day off.

We hit *Tide Pool* afterward to unwind and put back a few drinks. I was still a little amped up with adrenaline. But the scantily clad scenery was relaxing. The smell of chlorine and strawberry daiquiris filled the air. Pretty people frolicked in the outdoor pool, and we took in the scenery.

We were a few rounds in when a text from Gia buzzed my phone. *[How is your evening?]*

[It's better now.]

[I have a challenge for you.]

[A challenge?]

[A contest, really.]

[I'm listening.]

[If you can guess what color panties I'm wearing right now, I'll show them to you.]

[You know, your father's goons warned me to stay away from you.]

[Do you always do what you're told?]

[What do you think?]

[I think you're a man who does what he wants. Besides, my father's harmless.]

[Lol.]

[So, what color panties am I wearing?]

44

I texted: [You're not wearing any.]

[Congratulations. I'll be over to give you your prize shortly.]

[Meet me at the boat in half an hour.]

[Aye-aye, sir.]

I informed JD that my services were needed, and we left *Tide Pool*. He dropped me off at the marina and said, "I want a full report in the morning."

I gave him a mock salute, then jogged down to the *Avventura*. I crossed the passerelle, and Buddy waited for me eagerly at the salon door. I leashed him up and took him out for a quick walk before Gia arrived.

True to her word, she wasn't wearing anything under her skirt.

It didn't take long before her dress was on the deck. We made quite the racket as we explored various compartments on the ship. Her breathy moans tickled my ear, and her luscious form melted into mine.

After we'd worn ourselves out, we collapsed in my state-room, hot and sweaty, as it should be. It was a helluva cardio routine, better than any treadmill or exercise bike. My heart pounded, and pleasure chemicals swirled. Gia curled up beside me and all was right with the world.

It was a good way to unwind and forget about my day.

"I like your sense of adventure," she whispered in my ear.

"Well, I am taking my life in my hands, seeing you," I joked.

She smacked my chest playfully. "Whatever. Dino's just jealous. He has a crush on me. My father didn't put him up to it. Trust me."

"Right, your dad's clean now," I said, thick with sarcasm.

"Surely we can think of other things to talk about besides alleged criminal activity? In fact, we don't have to talk at all." She planted her wet lips on mine and straddled my hips, ready to go again.

It didn't take much convincing. She was very persuasive.

I'm sure the yacht pitched and rolled more than any other in the marina.

In the morning, I woke to the delightful smell of fresh coffee and bacon wafting through the ship. I pried open a sleepy eye and pulled myself out of bed.

I hit the head, brushed my teeth, pulled on a pair of boxers, and made my way down to the galley. The pan sizzled and popped with bacon as Gia slaved over the grill. "I hope you like ham and cheese omelettes."

I smiled. "I think I'd like just about anything you cooked."

"Smart answer."

"I didn't figure you for the domestic type."

"I'm not, but it's fun to pretend every now and then." She smiled.

Gia dished up breakfast, and we ate on the sky deck, enjoying a beautiful morning. I sipped coffee and crunched on bacon while the sunlight warmed my face. A few gulls hung on the draft, and waves gently lapped against the hull. Not a bad way to start the day. Gia even bussed the table, taking the plates down to the galley.

"What did I do to deserve this?" I asked when she returned.

"Is it a crime to do something nice for someone you're fond of?" she replied with a warm smile.

"So, you're fond of me?"

"Don't let it go to your head, Deputy. But you have your merits."

I chuckled.

"I hope you're somewhat fond of me," she asked, fishing.

"You wouldn't be here if I wasn't."

She smirked.

"I was a little surprised you stuck around this morning."

"I didn't plan on it, but your bed is so comfortable. How could I resist?" She dug into her little purse and pulled out a lighter and a joint. "You mind if I smoke?"

"You realize that's still illegal here."

She rolled her eyes. "Pffft. Whatever. It's a harmless plant."

"That as it may be, I'm still a cop, and you can't do that here."

"You wouldn't arrest little old me, would you?" she asked in an adorably innocent way.

I stared at her, unflinching.

"Fine, I won't wake and bake." She stuffed the lighter and the joint back into her clutch. "You're more fun when you're drinking."

She stuck her tongue out at me playfully.

"What you do on your time is your business. But not here. Not on the boat. Sorry."

"Are you always so by-the-book?"

"Mostly."

"That's okay. I respect that. A man of principles." She sighed. "I guess I should get going before somebody starts wondering where I am."

She kissed me on the cheek before getting up. Her sweet breath tickled my ear when she whispered, "I had fun."

"So did I. Thanks for breakfast. Tell Dino I said hello."

She laughed.

I escorted her to the main deck. She gave me another kiss before slipping out of the salon and sauntering across the passerelle. I watched her strut down the dock. She glanced over her shoulder one last time and smiled, wiggling her fingers goodbye.

She was an interesting girl, no doubt about it.

I got dressed, took Buddy out for a run, then came back to the boat and worked out. It was my day off, after all, so I lounged around on the sky deck, soaking up the Florida sun.

Jack called. "I'm coming over. We're gonna take the boat out and do a little treasure hunting."

"Sounds like a plan. But maybe we should hunt around the boat, looking for that book."

Jack had written the coordinates of the shipwreck we found in a paperback of *20,000 Leagues Under the Sea,* which had since gone missing.

"I'm telling you, one of your questionable companions probably absconded with it," he said.

"Doubtful. Are you sure you didn't misplace it?"

"It was in a compartment in the wheelhouse."

Sheriff Daniels buzzed the other line.

"It's the sheriff. I'll call you back," I said before clicking over.

"I've completed my thorough investigation. The shooting was within protocol. You're back on duty."

"Gee, thanks," I said, feigning enthusiasm.

"Another girl went missing."

I groaned.

"I need you and that nitwit to get down to the station and talk to the girl who made the report."

"I'll be right there."

So much for a relaxing day.

I called JD back and filled him in. He swung by the marina a few minutes later, and we headed to the station.

We spoke with a cute young blonde named Maria Griffith in the conference room. She had long straight hair that was highlighted. Her light brown eyes and flawless natural skin cast a spell stronger than any love potion. Her nose and cheeks were speckled with freckles. She wore a black halter top and jean shorts.

"Tell us what's going on," I said.

"I haven't seen Clara in a couple days, and I'm really worried about her."

Daniels sat in on the interview.

"Who's Clara?"

"Clara Greenway. She's my best friend."

"Where did you last see her?"

"We had gone out to Angelfish island for a sandbar party. There was music and plenty of boats with kegs and daiquiri machines and margaritas. You know, typical stuff."

"So, you both had been drinking."

She nodded.

"We were having a great time, then Clara met these guys. She wanted to party with them. And I didn't really want to. They were kinda... not my type." She cringed with revulsion.

"Tell me about them," I said.

"Well, one was kinda cute in that redneck kind of way. But they just looked dirty. One was a little older. He had blondish gray hair and a mustache that went down to his chin. He was really old. Like in his 50s."

JD frowned at her.

"The other guy was mid 30s. They looked kind of trashy. But Clara kind of likes that."

"So, you met these guys. Then what?"

"They invited us on their boat. Clara wanted to go. They had beer and *other* things."

"Drugs?"

"I'm not into drugs. Clara likes to... *experiment*, shall we say."

"What kind of drugs?"

"Well, they were doing a little coke. Not me. I don't do coke."

Something told me this girl had done her fair share.

"But then they wanted to do the hard stuff."

"Heroin?" I asked.

Maria nodded.

"And that's when you left?"

"I tried to get Clara to leave with me. But she wouldn't go. She was already pretty buzzed. I think she wanted to bang the cute one." She made a disapproving face. "I told her that I was going to mingle, and I'd come back to check on her. I ran into some friends and lost track of time. When I went back to find her, they were gone. I stayed out there for a couple hours looking through the crowd for her, but I never found her or the boat."

"How did you get to Angelfish?"

"I rode out there with some girlfriends on some guy's boat.

"And where were your friends when this was happening?"

Maria shrugged. "They stayed for a while, but they wanted to go back early. Clara and I told them we'd find a way back to Coconut Key. I mean, we're cute girls. Who's not going to give us a ride?"

"Why are you just now reporting this?"

Maria shrugged. "I don't know. I thought you had to wait 72 hours before you could report a missing person."

I shook my head. "That's not true."

She looked crushed. "Really?"

"You remember these guys' names?"

She thought for a moment. "Sherman and Clayton. No Clyde."

The moment she spoke, a bell rang. Sherman and Clyde were the guys Dean Dodd alleged had taken Sadie Bradshaw from Bongo Key.

"Are you sure about that?"

Maria nodded. "Yeah, why. Do you know those guys?"

"They may be the same guys wanted in connection with a sex trafficking ring."

Maria gasped. "Are you serious?"

"You remember the name of their boat?"

She thought again for another moment. "Money Pit."

On my phone, I pulled up the sketches of Sherman and Clyde that our artist had done. I showed them to Maria. "Are these the guys?"

Her eyes rounded. "Yeah."

"You're sure?"

"Yeah, that's pretty spot on."

I exchanged a glance with JD and the sheriff.

"Let's find those bastards," Daniels said.

45

Denise searched the registration records for the *Money Pit.* Sure enough, it belonged to Shurman Powers. The unusual spelling kept him from appearing in prior searches for suspects named Sherman. Denise pulled up his DMV photo, and we showed it to Maria. Again, she confirmed he was the guy.

I asked Maria to text me a few photos of Clara Greenway. The pictures she sent were of the two on a night out—red plastic cups in their hands and glassy eyes. Clara was a pretty girl in her early 20s with dark hair, brown eyes, and an alluring figure. One glimpse, and you knew she liked to have a good time. She had that mischievous look in her eyes.

We headed across the island to the *Pirate's Cove* marina. It wasn't the nicest marina on the island, but still not cheap. We parked in the lot and hustled down to the dock, looking for the *Money Pit.* It was a 38-foot Valkyrie sport fish. Older, but in decent shape.

I banged on the hull and shouted, "Coconut County. Looking for Shurman Powers."

Footsteps rumbled across the deck inside. I couldn't see through the dark tinted windows of the salon.

A moment later, Shurman opened the salon door and poked his head out. He grumbled, "What do you want?"

"Looking for Clara Greenway. You know where I can find her?"

He shook his head. "I don't know anybody by that name."

"That's funny because her best friend said that you partied with her the other night at Angelfish."

Shurman froze. He stared at me with cold eyes. "I party with a lot of people."

"Take a look at this picture," I said, digging for my phone in my pocket. I launched the photos app and found Clara's picture. I displayed the image for him. "Maybe this might jog your memory."

Shurman took a cautious step out of the salon and marched across the cockpit to the gunwale. He took a brief glance at the picture. Without taking enough time to process, he said, "Never seen her before."

"Are you sure? Take another look."

"I meet a lot of people."

"The last time anybody saw Clara was aboard your boat."

"A lot of people came aboard the boat that night. I had a keg of beer, and I'm a generous guy." He forced a smile. "People love free alcohol."

"I heard you also gave out free drugs."

His face tensed. "I don't know anything about that."

"You're friends with a guy named Clyde, right?"

His eyes narrowed. "I don't know anything about this girl. I'm sorry I can't be of more help."

He turned around and walked back toward the salon door.

"Mind if we take a look around the boat?"

"You got a warrant?"

"Don't need one. Routine compliance inspection. Make sure you've got the necessary paperwork and safety equipment."

"I'm not at sea."

"You're on the water."

His jaw tightened.

We could technically search the boat, looking specifically for compliance items and nothing else. The Coast Guard was a different story. "I can get a warrant. I can get the Coast Guard out here. They don't need a warrant."

"I've got nothing to hide," Shurman said. "Come aboard."

We boarded and walked across the cockpit. He held the salon door for us as we stepped inside.

It was a 1991 Valkyrie with a 14-foot beam, powered by an inboard diesel. Wood paneling lined the bulkheads. There was a small settee to starboard and an entertainment center to port. Forward, on the port side, was a small galley with a full-size refrigerator. Opposite was a small dining area.

Down the forward companionway, there was a guest state-room on the port side, with an en suite on the starboard side. Beyond that was a forward V-berth.

"Feel free to look around," Shurman said. "Clara is not here."

"I'm surprised you remember her name," I said.

He tapped his head with his index finger. "I've got a good memory."

We stepped forward, moving toward the galley. I kept my hand palming the grip of my pistol. I had an uneasy feeling the moment I stepped into the salon. I kept one eye forward and one eye aft. "Anybody else aboard with you?"

"Nope. I live here alone." Shurman stood by the salon door with his arms folded.

"What about Sadie Bradshaw?"

He kept a tight face and swallowed hard. "I'm sorry, that name doesn't sound familiar."

"Right," I said. "You meet a lot of girls."

"The perks of owning a boat."

"Nice boat. A real chick magnet."

"It gets the job done."

I twisted the handle and pushed open the hatch to the guest stateroom. The bunk was disheveled, and clothes were scattered about. It was clear someone was living in the guest berth.

"I thought you said you lived alone," I shouted down the companionway.

Jack hovered in the galley, keeping an eye on Shurman.

The tension was thick.

46

Shurman said nothing.

I inched forward, grabbed the handle to the master stateroom, and pushed open the hatch.

Muzzle flash erupted from within, and the deafening clatter of gunfire rattled the bulkheads.

Bullets snapped past my ear, and I flattened myself against the bulkhead, drew my pistol, and returned fire. I squeezed the trigger twice. My pistol hammered against my palm. Gunpowder filled my nostrils.

I put two bullets into Clyde's chest. He fell against the bed and flopped against the bulkhead, leaving a crimson stain as he slumped to the deck.

More gunfire erupted as JD exchanged fire with Shurman.

I spun around and stormed aft. There was no doubt in my mind that Clyde was no longer a threat.

By the time I got to the salon, Shurman was down, clutching the gaping wound in his chest, blood seeping between his fingers.

JD advanced and kicked Shurman's weapon out of reach.

I kept my weapon aimed at him while JD knelt down and rendered aid.

Wisps of gun smoke still lingered in the air.

JD put pressure on the wounds while I dialed 911.

I needed Sherman alive if we were to have any hope of finding Clara Greenway.

My ears rang and everything was muted. I shouted to Jack, "You alright?"

"I think so."

I moved back down the companionway to the master stateroom. I kicked Clyde's weapon out of reach, then felt for a pulse in his neck.

His heart no longer pumped.

I moved back to the salon. Shurman writhed and moaned as JD tried to stem the tide of blood. The smell and haze of gun smoke lingered.

Distant sirens warbled.

EMTs arrived and took over. They started supplemental oxygen and a paramedic began IV fluids. They managed to stabilize Shurman. He was transferred from the boat and wheeled down the dock on a gurney.

JD washed the blood from his hands in the galley sink.

Brenda and the forensics team boarded. Dietrich started snapping photos. There were bullet holes in the bulkheads and plenty of blood splatter. It would all be used to corroborate our version of the events.

I pointed Brenda in the direction of the forward stateroom.

"Racking up the body count this week, aren't you?"

I shrugged innocently. "I didn't start this. These people made a conscious decision to shoot at me."

"These people don't make good decisions, do they?"

We continued to search the boat while the forensic team did their thing.

We found a horrific discovery.

In a storage compartment, there were several IDs, purses, cell phones, and various bits of jewelry from dozens of young girls. Clara Greenway's ID was among them. It was hard to get an estimate of just how many women these men had trafficked over the years. But it was no small number.

We left Brenda and the forensic team. Curious residents gawked from cockpits. As usual, Paris and her crew were on the scene.

"No comment," I said as I pushed past the camera.

She frowned at me.

We hopped into the Porsche and headed to the hospital. Shurman had been triaged and was in emergency surgery. I let the receptionist know that we needed to speak with the suspect as soon as he was able. *If* he was able.

It was a big *if*.

We hung out in the waiting room under the pale fluorescent lights with dozens of sick and injured. An old lady had a cannula of oxygen feeding her nostrils. A roofer had fallen from a ladder and broken his arm. A college kid coughed incessantly. Breaking news droned from a flatscreen near the ceiling.

It was almost two hours later when Dr. Parker stepped into the waiting area, wearing teal scrubs and a surgical mask covering his face. "He's gonna live, but he's a little out of it right now and not up to answering any questions. I'll have someone contact you when he's more lucid."

I thanked him, and we headed back to the station to fill out after-action reports. Due to the shooting, we had to surrender our duty weapons and were put on administrative leave again.

We headed back to *Diver Down* and took a seat at the bar. Teagan greeted us with a concerned face and two glasses of whiskey. She knew us well.

Her eyes rounded when she got a good look at JD. His Hawaiian shirt and beige cargo shorts were speckled with Sherman's blood.

"I saw on the news there was a shootout at Pirates' Cove. That's two in two days, Tyson."

I shrugged. "If these people would stop shooting at me..."

"I'm glad you guys are okay."

I filled her in on the details.

"Do you think there's a chance you can find any of those missing girls?"

"I hope so. It all depends on if this guy lives or dies and if he decides to talk."

"You guys want something to eat?"

"I'll take the blackened catfish," JD said.

I went with the garlic marinated grilled half chicken.

Jack hustled down to the *Avventura*, showered, and changed clothes. He returned just as Teagan clanked our entrées on the bar.

We chowed down, sipped whiskey, and ruminated on the case.

It was late the next afternoon when Dr. Parker called. "I think Shurman can handle a few visitors now. I hope you get what you need out of him."

I thanked him again, and JD and I headed back to the hospital. A heart monitor blipped bedside and a nasal cannula fed Shurman supplemental oxygen. His wrist was cuffed to the railing. He looked remarkably well for a guy who'd been shot twice.

His face twisted with a scowl as we entered the room.

Shafts of light filtered through the blinds, and the TV was tuned to an afternoon game show.

"Fuck you," Shurman said as we approached the bed.

"Nice to see you, too," I replied.

47

I dropped a dozen IDs of young girls on the bedside tray. They clattered and fanned out.

Concern filled Shurman's eyes.

"You look like a smart guy, Shurman," I said, trying to soften him up. He looked like a dumb ass. "I'm sure you realize the situation you're in."

His worried eyes stared at me.

"We can do this the easy way or the hard way. I'd start thinking about cooperating if I were you. The attempted murder of my partner is enough to put you away for life. The other charges are just gravy at this point. Tell me about Clara Greenway and these other girls and I'm sure the DA will take that into consideration."

Shurman said nothing.

"Murder, attempted murder, kidnapping, human trafficking, and countless other charges. You can take your chances, but I don't think you'll like the results."

He wanted to defend himself, but Shurman remained silent. We stared at each other for a moment.

I found Clara Greenway's driver's license in the pile and held it up. "Still want to tell me you don't know who she is?"

His eyes surveyed her ID.

"I know you think I'm a bad guy, but I'm trying to help you. This is a one-time opportunity. You're not dumb enough to let that pass you by, are you?"

He continued to give me the silent treatment.

"Where are the girls now? I mean, you sell them, don't you? You pick up these wayward girls. Some of them are homeless, some of them come from broken families. Others are just looking to party or get away from their parents. You feed them drugs, get them strung out, then you sell them to somebody else who brokers them out. You're gonna take the fall while that broker walks away scot-free. How do you feel about that?"

Shurman's face tensed, and the wheels turned behind his eyes.

"Doesn't seem fair that they should continue to live free off your hard work." I paused. "You take a large portion of the risk, don't you?"

Shurman said nothing.

"No offense, but you don't look like the kind of guy with international contacts or the resources to run a large sex trafficking operation. You and Clyde were pulling girls here and there, making a decent living, but you probably spent it as fast as you got it."

Shurman pressed the call button. An instant later, a nurse's voice crackled through the tiny speaker. "How can I help you?"

"These gentlemen are disturbing me," Shurman said. "I need my rest."

"Nice try, Shurman," I said. "I'm not leaving here without answers."

The nurse entered the room a moment later. "Okay, gentlemen. It's time to leave."

I flashed my badge. "Call security. Call the Sheriff's Department because I'm not leaving unless someone drags me out of here or he starts talking. If you knew what this man did, you'd let us stay here as long as it takes to wrangle information from him. Girls' lives are at stake."

She hesitated for a moment, and her eyes flicked from me to Shurman, then back again. "I'm sorry, I must have stepped into the wrong room."

She turned around and darted out of the unit.

A thin smirk tugged my lips.

I lorded over Shurman. "If you hadn't noticed, people don't look too highly on abusers of underage girls. Just wait till you get to prison. They don't treat guys like you well in the big house. They'll put you in a unit with all the other perverts or put you in protective custody—23-hours a day in a 6x8 cell. You'll get maybe 30-45 minutes in an outdoor cage every day. If you're lucky, you might get a little sunlight on your face. But that's the extent of the world that you'll ever see again." I paused. "I've got an eyewitness that will testify that you took Sadie Bradshaw from Bongo

Key. Apparently, you guys had an arrangement with Fenton."

Fenton was a *spiritual guru* who abused and manipulated his followers.

I continued, "We found Sadie's body buried on Barracuda Key. She had a lethal amount of heroin in her system. I'm guessing that she was in your care and OD'd. That's murder, my friend."

Beads of sweat misted on his forehead, and his cheeks reddened. He was silent for a long moment as he contemplated his options. "I'll give you a name if you can guarantee that I won't do any time."

I laughed. "You're gonna do time, Shurman. There's no way around that. But you'll work with me if you ever want to breathe free air again. Otherwise, you will die in prison. I have no doubt in my mind."

48

"I swear to God, I'll put another bullet in you if you don't start talking," JD said.

He might have been serious too.

I think Shurman got the point.

"Wanderlust."

"What's that?" I asked.

"A superyacht. That's where you might find some of the girls."

JD nudged my elbow. "We've seen that boat before. On the way back from Barracuda Key."

"Who owns it?" I asked Shurman.

"I don't know. I just dealt with a guy named Dino."

My eyes rounded with surprise. "The same Dino that works for Vinnie Farina?"

"I don't know who he works for. He's the guy who paid me."

"How much?"

"50K a girl."

My jaw tightened. That's all a human life was worth to these people.

"If you're holding back on me…"

"That's it. That's all I know. Now you better cut me a sweet deal."

"If this pans out, I'll see what I can do."

He frowned at me.

I called Denise as we rushed out of the room and raced down the pastel hallways toward the elevator. "I need you to pull registration records for *Wanderlust*."

We hustled through the antiseptic hallways. Ventilators wheezed, and heart monitors blipped, the sounds spilling out from patient rooms.

"This is interesting. It says here that *Wanderlust* is registered to Michael Austin Williams."

My brow lifted with surprise. "Where is it docked?"

"According to the records, Sandpiper Point."

We took the elevator down to the first floor, then hustled to the parking lot and hopped into the Porsche. We sped across the island toward *Sandpiper Point*. It was an upscale marina full of new money—tech types, doctors, lawyers, crypto millionaires.

I called Megan Williams along the way. "Tell me about your husband's boat, the *Wanderlust*."

She stammered. "My husband doesn't have a boat named *Wanderlust*."

"There's one titled in his name."

"There must be some kind of mistake. The only boat we have is an 82-foot SunTrekker docked right behind the house."

"You're telling me he doesn't have an 87-meter Baldinotti at Sandpiper Point?"

"Not that I'm aware of, but maybe there are things he was keeping from me."

I was beginning to suspect there were quite a few things he was keeping from her.

We pulled into the parking lot at *Sandpiper Point*, hopped out, and hustled down the dock, looking for the *Wanderlust*. We scoured the slips but didn't find the superyacht. A boat that size wouldn't be hard to miss, even at *Sandpiper Point*.

Daniels called amid our search. "Tango One spotted them this side of Angelfish Key. Get your asses down to the station. I'll have the Coast Guard meet us there and do a compliance inspection."

"We're on our way," I said.

We climbed into the convertible and zipped to the station. Daniels had the engines fired up in the patrol boat, and we hustled down the dock to join him.

The sheriff idled out of the marina, then brought the boat on plane. The aluminum patrol boat crashed against the swells, and the engines howled, spitting a frothy white wake. The wind whipped across the bow, and the setting sun glimmered the water. The pastel sky, painted in hues of pink and orange, looked like a postcard.

By the time we reached the *Wanderlust*, the sun had dipped below the horizon. The boat was the epitome of luxury. It was massive in scale and almost looked like an ocean liner.

JD's eyes were full of boat envy as we drew near.

Daniels coordinated with the Coast Guard patrol boat, and we both converged on the superyacht at the same time.

A petty officer shouted into a megaphone. "United States Coast Guard. Prepare to be boarded for a safety inspection. Are there any weapons on board?"

A cocktail party was in progress with the guests in evening wear. We pulled to the swim platform and tied off.

"No weapons," a man shouted back.

We boarded the yacht and stormed the steps to the aft deck with the Coast Guard.

It wasn't a large party. Maybe half a dozen men with pretty young girls on their arms. Wine glasses dangled from manicured fingers, and all the girls had a thin hollow gaze about them.

I knew right away that some of these girls were on the missing list.

49

The yacht looked futuristic with sleek curves and windswept lines. The aft deck was home to a large sun-pad and a sunken bar with built-in seating. A moulded-in sunshade covered the space. Stairs on either side led to the upper deck. It was the perfect area for entertaining.

The gentlemen looked uneasy. The girls, uncertain.

I saw a familiar face.

"You got a warrant?" Enzo asked, emerging from the glass double doors that opened to the gymnasium. I'm talking a full gym with treadmills, exercise bikes, dumbbells and machines. Floor-to-ceiling mirrors on the forward bulkhead made the large compartment seem even bigger.

"Don't need one," Petty Officer Cruz said. "Just a routine safety inspection. Are you the owner?"

"No."

"Is the owner on board?"

"The owner's deceased," I muttered.

"What's your relationship to the deceased?" Petty Officer Cruz asked.

"He's a dearly departed friend," Enzo said, pretending to be deeply moved. He placed his hand on his heart. "He loaned the boat to me before he passed, and I saw no urgent need to return it. God rest his soul."

Officer Cruz was unamused. "I'll need to see your license and boat registration."

"I can assure you, everything's in order," Enzo said.

"We'll need to check life preservers, flares, fire extinguishers, etc."

Cruz knew exactly why we were here. The safety inspection was just an excuse. He nodded to his men, Fletcher and Huckabee. They pushed into the gym and searched the ship.

I hadn't seen Dino yet, but the two were never far apart. I wondered who else might be on board. Perhaps Vinnie himself.

I approached one of the girls and looked into her eyes. It was clear to me that she was on some type of substance. Her pupils were dilated, and she was numb to the world. She wore a nice black taffeta strapless cocktail dress that showed off her elegant shoulders. She was all dolled up with heavy eyeshadow. But it was all window dressing. She was empty inside.

"What's your name?" I asked.

"Crystal," she replied.

"Is that your real name?"

She hesitated. "Yeah."

"You have any ID?"

"I don't have to show you my ID."

"Yeah, you do."

"I don't have it on me."

I pulled out my phone and showed her a picture of Clara Greenway. "Have you ever seen this girl before?"

Her eyes flicked to Enzo, then back to the picture. "No. She doesn't look familiar."

She was lying.

I asked Enzo, "Want to tell me what's going on here?"

"Just a booze cruise with friends."

"I don't think these girls are old enough to drink."

"As far as I know, everyone aboard is over 21."

Petty Officer Fletcher poked his head out of the glass doors. "Sheriff, I think you'll want to see this."

He motioned us inside.

Cruz stayed on the aft deck with Enzo and the guests. Petty Officer Glover stayed aboard the patrol boat.

We followed Fletcher through the gymnasium and moved down a forward companionway. The hardwood flooring had intricate designs. The passage had crown molding and recessed lighting. It curved around a central compartment, and the bulkheads were lined with cream-painted wood paneling. 48x36 framed black and white prints of athletes engaged in various water sports hung on the bulkheads—jet skiing, water skiing, and surfing.

We passed through a door with a golden Greek pattern and stepped into another passageway. This passage had marble floors with black trim. There were Greek columns and more cream-painted wood-paneled bulkheads. Wall sconces illuminated the passageway.

I'd never been aboard a private boat as luxurious.

The interior was handcrafted by the famous Italian designer *Cavallo*.

We continued to follow Fletcher down the companionway, past a massage parlor and a day head to the main receiving lobby. An exquisite staircase spiraled to the upper deck and down below.

Fine art hung on the bulkheads and I swear I saw a small Picasso. This place was insane.

We made a short jog around the staircase and continued forward to a port-side guest stateroom where Officer Huckabee waited.

I shouldn't have been shocked at what I saw, but it still came as a surprise.

The Honorable Judge Echols stood by the hatch to the stateroom, looking disheveled. His hair was tousled, and it looked like he'd done a rush job of getting dressed. His shirt was half-tucked into his trousers, his tie was missing, and his coat was still in the stateroom.

"What is the meaning of this interruption?" Echols said in a blustery voice.

Fletcher muttered in my ear. "We found him in the stateroom with the girl. I think that's one of your missing persons."

Daniels had sent the Coast Guard crew pictures of the missing girls.

I looked past the judge, into the stateroom, at a girl huddled in bed with covers concealing her tender form.

It was Zoe Brooks.

It didn't take a rocket scientist to figure out Echols had been under the sheets with her.

"Judge, are you aware of the fact that your little friend in there has been reported missing?" I asked.

His face reddened. Flustered, he fumbled for words. "I had no such knowledge. I was merely having a conversation with her."

"A conversation?"

"Judge, I need you to put your hands against the bulkhead," Daniels said. "You're under arrest."

"That's preposterous. You can't arrest me. You have no right to search this vessel other than for compliance issues."

"I think you know better than that," Daniels said. He pointed to the Coast Guard. "They can search a vessel for any reason or no reason at all. Against the bulkhead, Judge. Now!"

Echols gave an indignant huff but complied.

Daniels usually played his cards close to his chest and didn't often wear his emotions on his sleeve, but I swear I saw a smile on his face as he slapped the cuffs around the judge.

I poked my head into the stateroom. "Zoe Brooks?"

She looked at me with terrified eyes and nodded.

"Get dressed. You're going home."

A moment after I pulled the hatch shut to give her some privacy, gunfire erupted on the aft deck. The chaos echoed throughout the ship.

50

I drew my weapon and moved down the companionway toward the stern. I held up at the entrance to the gym and surveyed the skirmish.

Bullets crisscrossed the deck.

The glass doors shattered.

Shards of glass rained to the deck and sparkled like diamonds.

Guests and girls dove for cover as Enzo blasted at Petty Officer Cruz.

Shrieks and screams filled the air.

Blood splattered, and the two went down.

The unmistakable whine of a helicopter spooling up seeped through the ship, emanating from the helipad on the massive foredeck.

Fletcher and Huckabee advanced through the gym toward Cruz and gave aid.

I spun around, sprinted down the passageway, and vaulted up the spiral staircase. I darted across the upper deck lobby, pushed onto the side deck, and sprinted toward the fore-deck. As I reached the pool—yes, a pool—I saw a black Dynocopter on the pad, rotor blades swirling. At $2.8 million, it was a light, nimble craft with a shrouded tail rotor. It was a favorite among the super-rich.

I took aim at the craft and raced past the pool as it lifted from the deck.

Rotor wash blasted the area.

The sleek craft was capable of holding a pilot and four passengers. It had a range of 430 nautical miles and a service ceiling of 23,000 feet. More than capable enough of reaching the Bahamas.

Whoever was in charge of this operation was about to slip away.

This probably wasn't a smart thing to do, but I crouched low and sprinted toward the helicopter as it hovered over the deck. I leaped into the air and grabbed onto the starboard skid.

Before long, my feet dangled above the deck.

It didn't take long for me to realize what a really bad idea this was. I pulled myself up and hooked my arm around the skid at the elbow. I could hold this position for longer with less strain.

The pilot banked the helicopter and angled the craft over the water. The sun had long since vanished, and there was nothing but miles of inky blackness.

Tango One hovered nearby, rotor blades thumping. The county helicopter chased the small craft into the abyss.

The Dynocopter's engine howled, and the wind whipped around the fuselage, stinging my eyes.

Technically, Tango One could follow the Dynocopter until we were out of state waters. I'm sure they would follow beyond that. But I had no doubt these clowns were headed to international waters in an attempt to escape.

A fall from this height might be survivable.

Might.

But we were quickly passing the point of no return. The helicopter ascended, and any fleeting thoughts I had of dropping into the water below vanished.

Needless to say, I was fully committed. I had pushed in all the chips and had to play out my hand, no matter what I was dealt.

I didn't know how much longer I could maintain my grip, but I was pretty sure I would exceed my ability in no time. 15 or 20 minutes hanging onto a skid several thousand feet above the ocean is incredibly draining—mentally and physically. My heart punched my chest, and my arm burned. It would go numb before too long.

The craft had two doors on each side, fore and aft. Since it was mainly used for transporting guests to and from the yacht, the pilot flew from the left side, leaving the front right open for passengers. All the controls were on the left side only, keeping the collective on the pilot's left, away from any accidental adjustment by passengers.

The rear passenger door slid open, and a pistol aimed in my direction.

Not exactly what I wanted to see at that particular moment. I had enough trouble hanging onto the skid. I didn't need some jackass shooting at me, but it kinda goes with the turf.

Muzzle flash flickered as Dino blasted several rounds. He fired left-handed, angling his arm out the door while he held on with the other. I was pretty sure he was right-handed. Fortunately, he was less accurate this way.

The bullets snapped past my ear, and one sparked the skid, inches from my arm.

I drew my pistol, took aim, and squeezed several rounds at Dino, hoping my left arm didn't turn to rubber in the process.

My bullets caught him in the upper left quadrant of his chest. The impact spun him, and he slumped back in the seat.

One of my bullets must have severed the brachial plexus—the nerve bundle near the shoulder that provides motor function to the arm. His weapon fell to the deck.

I didn't know if Dino was alive or dead. I couldn't really see from this angle. But he certainly wasn't in optimal health.

I holstered my pistol, then flung my leg onto the skid, and managed to pull myself up. I grabbed the step rail just below the door, and soon, I was standing on the skid, holding onto the step rail above. I grabbed onto the door handle for stability, then inched forward toward the doorway.

Dino lay slumped in his seat, bleeding out. I grabbed his jacket and yanked the bastard out.

He tumbled from the craft, whacked his head on the skid, and fell into the abyss.

I was shocked to see who was sitting beside him.

Muzzle flash illuminated the cockpit as the pilot angled a pistol toward me and took a few shots.

I ducked for cover, flattening myself against the fuselage, then returned fire. My bullet plowed through the back of his seat and drilled through his chest.

Crimson blood splattered the front window.

This was not a good scenario.

51

A helicopter is *dynamically unstable*. Without constant input from the pilot, all hell will break loose.

With a bullet through the pilot, things became unstable rather quickly. The helicopter banked to the left and began to yaw.

Dino's pistol that rested on the deck slid across the fuselage as the craft rolled. It glided right into the grasp of Gia, who scooped it up. She had been sitting next to Dino before I pulled him out of the helicopter.

She aimed the pistol at me as I climbed into the rear passenger compartment.

"I hope you know how to fly this thing," she shouted over the whine of the engine.

There wasn't time for small talk.

I climbed to the front and shoved the pilot out. He tumbled into the abyss, and I took his seat just as the helicopter was beginning to spiral.

A helicopter has three main controls. The *cyclic* controls the main rotor and adjusts the pitch and roll. Pull it left to go left, right to go right. Forward will nose the craft down and descend slightly. Pulling back on the cyclic will nose the craft up.

The *collective* adjusts power through rotor blade pitch collectively, which will increase or decrease altitude. In essence, pull up on the collective to increase power and altitude. Lower the collective to decrease altitude.

Two foot pedals control the yaw. Because of the rotational force of the main rotors, helicopters will spin without anti-torque adjustment.

I stabilized the helicopter rather quickly and banked us around toward Coconut Key.

Gia scooted to the right side of the copter and kept the pistol aimed at me. "I'm sorry, but Coconut Key is not in our travel plans today."

"Where did you have in mind?"

"One of the islands in the Bahamas, perhaps. Unless I can make other arrangements."

"Then what. You'll be on the run."

"I have money. Money buys favors."

"How long have you been in charge of Vinnie's operation?" I asked.

"For quite some time now. When I told you my father was clean, I meant it."

There was a reason nobody could ever get anything on Vinnie. They'd been focusing on the wrong person.

"I don't suppose you want to help me get away? You'll have plausible deniability. I forced you at gunpoint."

"Sorry. I can't do that."

"I didn't think so, but it was worth a try. I'll be honest with you, I feel really bad it's come to this. I was quite fond of you, Deputy. You were good fun. But all things come to an end."

"All things have their season."

"Turn us around and head to the Bahamas," she demanded.

"And if I don't?"

She was silent for a moment.

"Unless you can fly this helicopter, I'd think twice about shooting me."

"I'm not going to jail, Deputy."

"You trafficked young girls. How could you do that?"

"Most of these girls' lives were going nowhere. They came from abusive homes. I gave them first-class accommodations, designer clothes, gourmet meals, and the finest luxury items. I don't really see what the big deal is. They'd be giving themselves away for free to some inexperienced douchebag. They make good money. I give them a percentage of all earnings."

"So, you're giving them a real career path," I snarked.

"They can leave anytime they want."

I didn't believe it for a second. "Right, after they pay off their debt to you? Which they will never be able to do. How can they leave when you've got them strung out? How many girls have you actually let go?"

Gia's face tightened. "Turn this helicopter around. Now!"

Her finger tightened around the trigger. She aimed the barrel of the pistol away from my head and squeezed.

The deafening bang rattled my brain, and the bullet snapped in front of my face, drilling a hole through the windshield. My ears rang, and everything sounded muffled for a moment. The tangy scent of gunpowder filled the cabin, and wind whistled through the new hole in the windshield.

"I'm not playing around, Tyson."

"I see that."

I pulled on the cyclic and angled the Dynocopter east. "What happens to these girls when they get past their prime?"

"Sometimes I find them a forever home. Sometimes they get traded to the minor leagues."

My jaw tightened, and I seethed with anger. Her callous disregard for human life was appalling. "Doesn't sound like they have much choice in the matter."

"Your pistol, Deputy. I want you to remove it from its holster and toss it out the window. Slowly and carefully, with your thumb and index finger only. Use your left hand."

There was a small camera portal in the window. I slid it open then delicately reached for my weapon.

"Easy, Tyson."

"Shoot me, and we both die."

"We were both dead the day we were born. We each have a number, and when our time is up, it's up."

"I don't know about you, but I'd rather not go today."

"Me neither. See, we have so much in common."

I reached my left hand slowly toward the weapon. As I began to pull it from its holster, I yanked the cyclic hard.

The abrupt movement rolled the helicopter and sent Gia tumbling against the right bulkhead.

52

Gia squeezed the trigger as she tumbled to the bulkhead. Another bullet rocketed across the compartment. It snapped past me and made another hole in the windshield.

Like lightning, I drew the pistol with my left hand. I had to rotate my wrist and make a small adjustment as I pulled it from the holster. I took aim and fired off two rounds.

The bullets smacked her chest, making an unmistakable thud.

She groaned like she'd been punched in the stomach, and blood spattered the bulkhead. Her eyes rounded with disbelief as crimson gushed from the gaping wounds.

It tore me up to do it. I really liked her—before I knew what kind of monster she was.

With the last bit of strength, she aimed her pistol at me and tried her best to squeeze the trigger.

She didn't have enough left in her to complete the job.

Her hand fell, and the gun tumbled away. Gia slumped as the last breath of life escaped from her pretty lips that were now drizzled with crimson.

The tinny, metallic scent of blood filled the cabin, and a wave of sadness washed over me.

I holstered the pistol and banked the helicopter around. I got on the radio, contacted Tango One, and let them know I had the situation under control.

I found my way back to the *Wanderlust*. It was a massive ship, but at night, pitching and rolling in the vast ocean, it looked like a tiny speck on the water.

Landing a helicopter on a superyacht at night in relatively calm seas is nothing like trying to set an FA-18 Hornet down on the deck of an aircraft carrier amid 30-foot swells. But it will demand your full attention.

I circled the LZ to recon the area, then made my approach. I lowered the collective, applying increasing amounts of left pedal, and hovered over the deck. It rose and fell with the swells, and I had to time the landing just right.

The skids finally touched down.

I killed the engine, hopped out, and felt relieved to have my feet on something firm. I gave a last look at Gia's body before walking away with a frown.

By this time, first responders swarmed the *Wanderlust*. Several Coast Guard boats were on the scene, and Petty Officer Cruz had been medevaced.

The guests were taken into custody, and the victim support unit handled the girls. Many of them had nowhere else to go and weren't particularly keen on leaving the luxurious surroundings or their drug- fueled lifestyle. Sometimes captives don't want to leave. They form a strange bond with their captors.

Dietrich snapped photos, and Brenda examined Enzo's remains. I found her on the aft deck and told her she had another decedent to evaluate in the helicopter.

"You're one crazy-ass son-of-a-bitch," JD said to me, relief filling his eyes.

"That means a lot coming from you. Thank you."

"I was pretty well convinced that was the last time I was going to see you."

"I guess I haven't run out of lives just yet." I paused. "You're not gonna believe who was in charge of this show."

I told Jack about Gia, and his jaw dropped.

"That's a damn shame. Pretty girl. You sure can pick 'em. I told you not to get involved with her."

I scowled at him playfully.

"Well, there is a bright side to all of this," JD said. "Can you say *civil asset forfeiture?*" The wheels turned behind his eyes. "The county will confiscate this boat and auction it off."

"Oh, no," I said, knowing exactly what he was thinking.

"We can at least bid. It would be the steal of the century. Do you know what a yacht like this retails for?"

It was an impressive boat, to be sure.

To placate Jack, I said, "We'll cross that bridge when we come to it."

We wrapped up at the scene and headed back to Coconut Key with Sheriff Daniels aboard the patrol boat. Judge Echols and the other prisoners were processed, printed, and interrogated. Echols was smart enough to keep his mouth shut, but he wasn't going to get out of this one.

Zoe Brooks gave a full statement chronicling how Axel had gotten her hooked on heroin and sold her to the mob. In order to get her routine fix, she had to do unspeakable things.

The victim support unit would assist in her rehab, and her testimony would seal the judge's fate.

Vinnie avoided prosecution.

Clara Greenway was found in a below-deck stateroom so doped up she couldn't move. It was a miracle she didn't OD.

A deep dive into Austin's books revealed a money laundering operation and straw purchases for the mob that included the superyacht. His murder for hire was a random coincidence that threw a wrench in Gia's operation.

At the station, we filled out after-action reports, then headed to Oyster Avenue to blow off steam.

We'd earned a little break.

We caught the tail end of *Thought Police* at *Distortion*. It was a small rock'n roll club with a decent sound system and cheap drinks. Live music every night of the week. New acts started on Mondays at 7 PM and worked their way up to headlining Saturdays.

We were looking for an opening act for an upcoming show at *Sonic Temple.*

The minute I had a clear view of the stage, my eye was drawn to the guitarist. She was good looking, and could shred on guitar. But that wasn't what caught my attention.

53

The guitarist, Jessie Jams, was playing Dizzy's stolen axe. I was sure of it. It was unmistakable.

I had more than a passing interest in speaking with her after the show. All of *Wild Fury's* gear had been stolen over the holidays, along with several other bands' gear from the practice space.

I was intent on catching the little bastards.

Some of the other bands had damn near folded. Gear was expensive and musicians often had little money. Jack didn't make a big deal out of it, but he bought gear for the bands in the warehouse that had been wiped out. Even the bands he didn't like.

We hung out, had a drink, and waited for Jessie to get off stage. I didn't think she'd stolen the axe herself, but she could tell me who she purchased it from. That would be a start.

My phone buzzed with a call from the reformed gangster, Tony Scarpetti. I answered and shouted over the music, "Hang on. Let me get where I can hear you."

I stepped outside to the patio.

"You sure know how to make friends," Scarpetti said.

"It's a natural gift," I joked.

"Vinnie Farina put a contract on you. Watch your back."

"Thanks for the heads-up."

"You didn't think you'd kill his daughter and not suffer any repercussions, did you?"

Ready for more?

The adventure continues with Wild Jewel!

Join my newsletter and find out what happens next!

AUTHOR'S NOTE

Thanks for all the great reviews!

I've got more adventures for Tyson and JD. Stay tuned.

If you liked this book, let me know with a review on Amazon.

Thanks for reading!

—*Tripp*

TYSON WILD

Wild Ocean

Wild Justice

Wild Rivera

Wild Tide

Wild Rain

Wild Captive

Wild Killer

Wild Honor

Wild Gold

Wild Case

Wild Crown

Wild Break

Wild Fury

Wild Surge

Wild Impact

Wild L.A.

Wild High

Wild Abyss

Wild Life

Wild Spirit

Wild Thunder

Wild Season

Wild Rage

Wild Heart

Wild Spring

Wild Outlaw

Wild Revenge

Wild Secret

Wild Envy

Wild Surf

Wild Venom

Wild Island

Wild Demon

Wild Blue

Wild Lights

Wild Target

Wild Jewel

Wild...

CONNECT WITH ME

I'm just a geek who loves to write. Follow me on Facebook.

www.trippellis.com

Made in United States
North Haven, CT
14 January 2022

14799259R00171